Praise f[or...]

"The re[...]
story ha[...]"
—*Fort Worth Star-Telegram*

"Mr. Fessier develops the age-old struggle of good and evil with all the clarity and dispatch of a hard-boiled detective novel."
—*Kansas City Star*

"A book that it is an experience to read. You live an eternity in 200 pages."
—*London Observer*

"I read it last night in one grand gulp."
—J. B. Pricstley

"The effect is as surprising and stimulating as a smack in the hoot-nanny with an ice-cold wash cloth."
—Bruce Catton

"a bizarre and extraordinary piece of writing"
—*Madison Capital Times*

"a sinister, fascinating book"
—*Pittsburgh Post-Gazette*

"Readers may find it disturbing and perplexing, but they will find it engrossing . . ."
—*St. Louis Star-Times*

FULLY DRESSED
AND IN
HIS RIGHT MIND
by
Michael Fessier

Introduction by
David Rachels

Staccato
CRIME

AN IMPRINT OF STARK HOUSE PRESS

FULLY DRESSED AND IN HIS RIGHT MIND
By Michael Fessier
Copyright May 20, 1935 by Michael Fessier
Copyright Renewed June 5, 1962
"Sex Murder in Cameron," "Nice Bunch of Guys," and "The Faceless Man"
copyright 1953 by Flying Eagle Publications.
All works reprinted with the permission of the author's estate.

Published by Staccato Crime
An imprint of Stark House Press
1315 H Street
Eureka, CA 95501, USA
griffinskye3@sbcglobal.net
www.starkhousepress.com

Introduction ©2022 by David Rachels

All rights reserved under International and Pan-American Copyright
Conventions.

ISBN: 979-8-88601-009-1
Staccato Crime: SC-005

All Staccato Crime titles are edited and produced
by David Rachels and Jeff Vorzimmer.
Book series design by *jcaliente!design*, Austin, Texas

This is a work of fiction. Names, characters, places and incidents are either the
products of the author's imagination or used fictionally, and any resemblance to
actual persons, living or dead, events or locales, is entirely coincidental.

Without limiting the rights under copyright reserved above, no part of this
publication may be reproduced, stored, or introduced into a retrieval system or
transmitted in any form or by any means (electronic, mechanical, photocopying,
recording or otherwise) without the prior written permission of both the
copyright owner and the above publisher of the book.

First Staccato Crime Edition: November 2022

CONTENTS

Introduction 7
Fully Dressed and in His Right Mind.................................. 15
Sex Murder in Cameron... 137
Nice Bunch of Guys 148
The Faceless Man 155

Michael Fessier, 1934

Introduction

> In this city of fog and fish and shrimp and Chinamen, there dwells a sinister person who by some inward alchemy has succeeded in changing himself from a human being to a monster.
>
> —Laurence Dorgan

> I looked at the picture he'd painted and it was just a lot of colors. It didn't make sense.
>
> —John Price

Michael Fessier launches *Fully Dressed and in His Right Mind* like a hardboiled rocket with 12 sentences totaling 269 words and only one comma while the word *and* appears 25 times so the prose flies and flies with an occasional period allowing a quick breath but real rest not coming until clipped dialogue begins with sentence 13. This opening is thrilling, a stylistic tour de force, but Fessier's virtuoso velocity makes a promise that he will keep only on his own surprising terms. Readers will hurtle through *Fully Dressed and in His Right Mind* to discover that the novel is something different than its hardboiled opening may have led them to expect. Something strange. Something wonderful.

Of course, some noir fans may suspect that a "wonderful" novel is not for them. Fans love what they love, and to some, genre is a sacred contract between author and audience: Writers must follow the rules, even if the results end up all seeming the same. A memorable example: When I was a teenager, my after-school job was shelving books at the public library. Harlequin Romances were especially popular with some elderly female patrons, who would check them out dozens at a time. At some point while shelving Harlequins, I noticed pencil marks on their first pages. One first page might have a triangle in its upper left corner and a circle in its lower right. Another might have this triangle and circle and also a star in the middle of the page. Perplexed, I asked a coworker what it all meant. He said, "That's how the old ladies keep track of which ones they've read. You know they're all the same, right?"

Suffice to say, you will not need your personal pencil mark to remember that you have read *Fully Dressed and in His Right Mind*. Upon the novel's publication in May 1935, newspaper reviewers struggled to classify it for their readers, and the book's abstruse title—an allusion to Mark 5:15 and Luke 8:35—didn't help matters ("the title apparently has nothing to do with the content," groused the *St. Louis Star-Times*). The United Press described the novel in hopelessly broad terms as "a new style of writing." The *Green Bay Post-Gazette* did little better with "a new style of fiction . . . a caricature symphony of life." The hapless critic for the *Lancaster New Era*, after professing to have "no idea what it's about," labeled the novel "fantastic and tenuous" before advising, "You'd better read it yourself." But many critics were more helpful, and fairly consistent, in describing the novel as a hybrid: "fantasy, written in a hard-boiled style" (*Richmond News Leader*); "mysticism and unreality . . . combined with the trusty style of the James Cain-Dashiell Hammett reform school" (*Kansas City Star*); "hard-boiled horror sicklied o'er with whimsy" (*Chicago Daily Tribune*); "a mysteriously fused Edgar Allen *[sic]* Poe-Hans Christian Andersen" (*Lexington Herald*). But the dominant tone of the novel is neither fantastical nor whimsical. As the *Pittsburgh Post-Gazette* noted, "the novel as a whole is as unvarnished and realistic as a newspaper story."

The novel's fantastical elements are embodied in two characters. The first is a nameless, serial-killing old man with terrifying eyes. One character says of him, "He looks at me, you see, and his eyes grow bigger and bigger and then they grow small again and all of a sudden they turn green. . . . When his eyes go green on me I have the same feeling I had once when I come face to face with a rattlesnake raised up on his hind end and snapping his fangs at me." As noted by Robert D. Hare, creator of the Hare Psychopathy Checklist diagnostic tool, "Some people respond to the emotionless stare of the psychopath with considerable discomfort, almost as if they feel like potential prey in the presence of a predator." Another character sums up the old man's personality: "I figure he is an ordinary human being with an enormous capacity for evil. Somehow, his brain has been thrown out of gear and off its trolley and his mental processes are beyond our understanding." So, while the old man may resemble a shape-shifting monster, this is also a fair way of portraying a real-life psychopath.

The other fantastical character is the young woman Trelia, who serves as a quasi-femme fatale. At first she appears in and around a small lake in Golden State Park, and it seems that she might exist only there. Midway through the novel, however, she appears away from the lake and clothed for the first time: "She was dressed in something green and soft and she didn't wear a hat and her hair tumbled over her shoulders. . . . The green thing made her look as if she were dressed in part of the lake." Green connects Trelia with the old man, and appropriately so. The color's split symbolism dates to the end of the Middle Ages, when its traditionally positive associations—including youth, beauty, and love—were challenged by an association with the devil. As a result, shades of green were sometimes given names to reflect this duality, as in Middle French with its *vert gai* and *vert perdu*. Fessier, however, obscures any such differences with greens that are always simply "green" in keeping with the hardboiled directness of his narration. (One possible exception: Trelia's "green and soft" dress is later described as a "soft green dress," which could describe a soft shade of green, especially without an intervening comma.)

Though critics imagined great success for *Fully Dressed and in His Right Mind*—"It requires no gift of prophecy to predict with assurance that [it] will be a best seller," proclaimed the *Fort Worth Star-Telegram*—the book was soon forgotten and has been reprinted only once. During the noir paperback boom of the 1950s, Lion Books brought it back, though they had no idea—or, rather, no *good* idea—what to do with it. The cover of the 1954 Lion reissue features a clothed Trelia perched on a large rock in the middle of a small lake. We look at her over the shoulder of a man in a suit whose posture suggests surprise. The front cover announces, "A SHAPELY NYMPH TANGLES WITH TEMPTATION," and the back cover further promises, "men from all over the city . . . getting themselves involved with the nymph." These descriptions are absurdly misleading, but what could Lion do? Readers who bought this paperback probably wanted their 25 cents refunded, but if Lion had marketed a hardboiled-fantasy mash-up, would anyone have bought it at all?

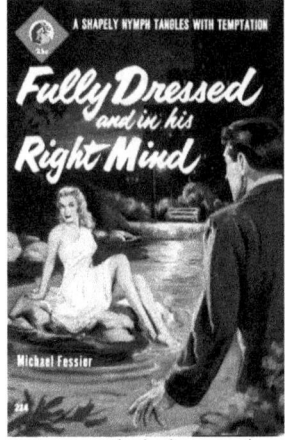

Lion paperback edition, 1954

As well, there is one great what-if: At some point—the exact date is unknown—Orson Welles planned a film of *Fully Dressed and in His Right Mind*. A partial draft adaptation survives, though it is unclear whether the work is by Welles alone or with collaborators. In either case, one wonders what Welles might have done with the novel (especially if given free rein) and whether that film might have sparked an ongoing audience for Fessier's work.

Michael Fessier (1905-1988) was a prolific writer but not a prolific novelist. His career took him from newspapers to magazines to movies to television with two novels as footnotes. (His second novel, 1948's *Clovis*, chronicles the adventures of a highly opinionated, multilingual parrot.) A California native, Fessier was 12 when his father abandoned the family, and at 13, he began working as a printer's devil for the *Bakersfield Californian*. After moving up to reporting jobs at other

California newspapers, Fessier began writing short stories for the pulps. Big breaks came in 1934 and 1935: He was a "discovery of the month" for *Esquire* magazine, and then MGM invited him to try writing screenplays, prompting him to quit his job as an editor for the *San Rafael Independent*. Fessier published over 200 short stories with the much-anthologized "That's What Happened to Me" serving for many years as a staple of high school English classes. He received credit for 29 screenplays with the best known being a pair of Fred Astaire-Rita Hayworth musicals—*You'll Never Get Rich* (1941) and *You Were Never Lovelier* (1942)—that he co-wrote with his screenwriting partner Ernie Pagano.

Fessier's Hollywood career came to an appropriate end for the author of the genre-bending *Fully Dressed and in His Right Mind*. According to Fessier's son, Michael Fessier Jr., his father's final screenplay was for the "interesting box-office bomb" *Red Garters* (1954), "a jokey surrealistic musical Western . . . that managed to end my father's and [Rosemary] Clooney's movie careers simultaneously." Fessier Jr. notes his theory that "in Hollywood one's bravest, most singular work is often what sinks your boat." Fessier Sr. finished his career writing for television shows such as *Bonanza, Lost in Space, Mister Ed, Gilligan's Island,* and *Alfred Hitchcock Presents.*

The dust jacket for the first edition of *Fully Dressed and in His Right Mind* observes, "The adventures of these characters are incredible and fantastic, yet they have a reality for the reader that is almost beyond comprehension. They never happened, never could happen, but it will be a very rare reader indeed who will not be so completely entranced by them that he will fail to finish the book in one exciting sitting." Indeed, the novel reads fast, not just because of the subject matter and prose style but also because the book is short. In rave reviews, the *Madison Capital Times* reported that "you gulp it down at a sitting," and the *Pittsburgh-Post Gazette* agreed that "most people will find themselves reading through in a single sitting."

But the book's brevity prompted at least one complaint. The *Chicago Daily Tribune*, after noting that the novel was expanded from Fessier's short story "The Man in the Black Hat," grumbled that "the result is no more a novel than was the original story. The book is really a 216 page long, short story." With this criticism in mind (unfair though it may be), this Staccato Crime edition of *Fully Dressed and in His Right Mind* also includes Fessier's three short stories from the great noir digest *Manhunt*: "Sex Murder in Cameron" (February 1953), "Nice Bunch of Guys" (May 1953), and "The Faceless Man" (June 1953). While these stories fall outside Staccato Crime's ordinary chronological window of 1899 to 1939, they serve as a fitting coda to Michael Fessier's too-brief career as a rule-breaking noir novelist.

David Rachels
Newberry, South Carolina

Notes on Sources

The Robert D. Hare quotation is taken from *Without Conscience: The Disturbing World of the Psychopaths Among Us* (Guilford Press, 1999), 208. Information on the symbolic history of the color green comes from Michel Pastoureau, *Green: The History of a Color* (translated by Jody Gladding; Princeton, 2014), 89. The description of Orson Welles' dalliance with *Fully Dressed and in His Right Mind* is based on Matthew Asprey Gear, *At the End of the Street in Shadow: Orson Welles in the City* (Wallflower, 2016), 79, 156. Michael Fessier's writing career is summarized from Michael Fessier Jr., "My Father, the Writer; or, Hollywood Is Forever," *LA Weekly*, 19-25 December 1997, 22-32. Fessier Jr. describes *Fully Dressed and in His Right Mind* as being "a distinctly strange work."

FULLY DRESSED AND IN HIS RIGHT MIND

1

I was standing in front of the *Herald* and somebody fired a shot and I saw a fat man turn slowly on one heel and fall to the sidewalk. Before I could get to him a crowd had gathered and they pushed and shoved and yelled and a police whistle blew and brakes squealed as drivers skidded their cars to stop and have a look at what was going on. Those who got near the body stood there and guzzled the sight. The fat man had a small blue hole in his head, and his mouth hung open and one eye looked right at you and the other was shut.

The people behind pushed the people in front and the people in front fought for their places and swore and tried to keep from stepping on the body. One fellow stepped on an opened hand and it curled up and the fellow shrieked and fought his way back into the middle of the crowd. The eye that had been open started to close slowly and a drop of blood formed in each nostril.

A couple of policemen shoved their way through the crowd and stood there looking at the body and blowing their whistles. Some more policemen came and pretty soon they formed a circle around the fat man. They swore at the crowd and waved their clubs and the crowd fell back but not very far.

The policemen kept asking if anybody'd seen who did it but nobody had.

I shoved my back through the crowd and started down the sidewalk and a man started walking alongside me.

"Hell of a note, wasn't it?" I asked him.

"Was it?" he asked.

"Didn't you see it?" I asked.

"Sure," he said. "I saw it."

"Wonder who did it," I said.

"I did," he said.

I looked at him. He wasn't smiling. He was smoking a cigar and squinting his eyes at the end of it.

"The hell you did," I said.

"Yes," he said. "I did it."

"You wouldn't try to kid me, would you?" I asked.

"Not unless it happened to be necessary," he said.

He was a little fellow and his clothes weren't very neat but still they weren't shabby. He had bushy white hair.

"You ought to be ashamed of yourself," I said. "A nice old man like you going out and getting gassed up on canned heat!"

"I'm not drunk," he said.

"All right," I said. "I won't argue with you. But don't go around repeating your story or some cop's liable to throw your pants in the klink just for the ducks of it."

"That would be too bad for the cop," he said.

I laughed.

"You don't mean to tell me you're one of those guys who eat cops for breakfast, do you?" I asked.

"I had no intention of creating such an impression," he said, "but as a matter of fact I did partake of a cop once."

"The hell you did," I said.

"He wasn't exactly a cop," said the little old man. "He was a British colonial officer and some African natives caught him away from his troops and killed him. They invited me to the dinner."

"Is that a fact?" I asked.

"It is," he said.

"Well now, and how do you like your British colonial officers, rare, medium, or well done?" I asked.

"Well done," he said, "although when you're dining with cannibals you take what you can get."

We'd come to an intersection and the light was against us and we stopped on the curbing.

"Well," I said, "at least you get on original jags, don't you?"

"I don't get on jags," he said.

"Maybe not," I said, "but it seems you drink a hell of a lot."

The light turned green and I stepped off the curbing.

"Good-by," I said, "and if I were you I'd scram back to wherever you came from before they catch you and throw you in the reform school or something."

He smiled and waved his cigar at me and I crossed the street. I started thinking about him and all of a sudden I realized there was something funny about him and I couldn't figure out what it was. I laughed and told myself to forget the old boy but I kept thinking about him.

2

Pretty soon all the cripples and blind men and loud-voiced kids, and moldy old ladies on the street corners were selling extras about the shooting and people were buying them and walking down the sidewalks reading them and banging into other people and getting themselves cursed. I bought one and stood in a doorway and read it and found out the man who'd been killed was the publisher of the *Herald* and his name was Albert E. Bagley. The paper I had was the *Herald* and it said probably he'd been killed on account of his stand against lawlessness and vice. Later I bought another paper and the fellow who wrote their story didn't seem to know anything about Bagley's being against lawlessness and vice because he didn't mention it anywheres in three and a half columns.

I went to a bar and got myself a salami sandwich and a glass of beer and stood up against the bar and talked to the bartender. He said the way he figured it it was a good idea somebody bumped off old man Bagley but he'd enjoy it more if he knew who did it. He didn't like mysteries, he said.

"How come you're in favor of him getting conked?" I asked. "What'd he do to you?"

"Nothing," he said.

"That's a good reason," I said. "A hell of a good reason. Why, if you'd killed him yourself and explained it to the cops they'd of done nothing whatsoever about it."

"Aw, he was an old crook," the bartender said. "Why, I bet that guy had a million dollars."

"More or less," I said. "You mean you didn't like old Bagley on account of he was rich."

"Sure," he said. "What better reason can you think of?"

"One or two," I said, "but we'll let it pass. Are you still on duty?"

"Sure," he said.

"Then give me a glass of beer," I said.

He got me the beer and went down the bar to talk to a fellow who agreed with him about what a good thing it was somebody'd killed Bagley. I took my sandwich and beer and sat down at a table and when I looked up there was the little old man with the bushy white hair.

"How do you do?" he said.

"Fine," I said. "Very fine. How come I've been in and out of San Francisco for years and never seen you and today you pop up everywheres I go?"

"I couldn't say," he said.

"Will you have a glass of beer?" I asked.

"I don't mind if I do," he said.

I called to the bartender and after he'd brought the beer I pointed to the little old man.

"By the way," I said, "this is the fellow that killed Bagley."

The bartender grinned.

"No!" he said.

"A fact," I said. "Doesn't he look the type?"

"He sure does," said the bartender. "A regular killer, ain't he? He your father?"

"I should say not," I said. "Why, if he'd been my father he'd have eaten me in a sandwich before I got to be five years old. He's tough, this lad is. It isn't everybody goes around pothunting publishers and getting away with it."

"You telling *me?*" said the bartender.

"Of course killing Bagley was just practice," I said. "He's in training for a massacre."

"Why, the old sonofagun!" said the bartender.

The little old man gave me a quick look, just a flash but I caught something that sent a chill leapfrogging up and down my spine. Then he picked up his beer and sloshed it around in his glass a second and all of a sudden threw it in the bartender's face. The bartender wiped his eyes and clenched his fist and stepped toward the little old man. He stood there with his fist held above his head and the little old man looked at him and slowly his fist relaxed and his arm fell to his side and he just stared pop-eyed.

The little old man got up and put a dime on the table and walked out without turning to look back. The bartender looked at me and gulped and his eyes bugged out like a frightened carp's.

"Jesus God!" he said.

3

When I went back to the bar, the bartender gave me a sour look and acted as if he'd just as soon not see me ever again. He served me and wiped the bar and washed some glasses and whistled to himself and didn't say anything to me.

"Lovely day, isn't it?" I said. "More damn fog."

"Yeah," he said. "I noticed it."

He started wiping a glass and gave me a funny look.

"Where's your friend?" he asked.

"You mean the little old guy?" I asked.

"Yeah," he said, "the little old guy."

"I don't know," I said. "That's the second time I ever saw him and I guess it'll be the last."

He looked suspicious.

"Sure that wasn't a gag?" he asked. "I mean about him swishing beer in my face?"

"If it was," I said, "it was his idea."

"Hell of an idea," he said.

"You held your temper pretty well," I said. "A lot of fellows would have taken a poke at him."

He looked at me in amazement.

"What the hell you think I was going to do?" he asked. "Shake his hand or something? Why, hell, man, I was going to paste the old geezer a good one."

"Why didn't you?" I asked.

"Yeah," he said. "Why didn't I?"

"Suppose you tell me," I said.

"He looked at me," the bartender said. "God-a'mighty, man! He *looked* at me."

"Yes," I said. "Go on."

He spread his hands out on the bar.

"That's it," he said. "That's all. He *looked* at me. Hell on a bike! What a look!"

"You mean something in his eyes stopped you?" I asked.

He sniffed.

"Ain't that what I been trying to tell you?" he asked. "Sure it was something in his eyes. I couldn't a hit him any more'n I could pat a snake on the head."

"What about his eyes?" I asked.

"Didn't you notice?" he asked. "They were green. Solid green and they glittered like a cat's do at night. Ugh!"

I had my drink and I remembered there was something funny about the little old man. Something that bothered me and I couldn't figure out why.

"Now I know," I said. "Now I remember. It was his eyes."

"Sure," said the bartender, "it was his eyes."

4

It was late and I'd had two cognacs more than enough and I was tired. I walked up the Stockton Street tunnel to avoid the climb up Powell Street. A couple of canned-heat bums struck me up and I turned them down and a floozie cooed at me and I told her to go to hell and she snarled at me and I made a pass at her and she went away. When I got home I turned on the light and started for the kitchen to get a drink of water and then I stood stock still in the middle of the room and my eyes bugged out so they hurt.

The little old man was sitting in my chair reading the *Satyricon*. He looked up at me and back at the book and turned a page.

"Good evening," he said.

"What the hell you doing here?" I asked.

"Reading," he said. He pointed to the book. "I suppose you read this for sex excitement," he said.

"Any sex excitement I want I don't have to get out of a book," I said. "What are you doing here?"

He put the book on the table and looked around him.

"Nice place," he said. "I like your etchings. Unsworth's, aren't they?"

"Yes," I said, "but would you mind telling me how come you're here and how you got in?"

"Why, I just walked in," he said.

"The door was locked," I said.

"It isn't now," he said.

"What are you, a burglar?" I asked.

"Yes," he said. "Sometimes."

"What if I'd call the cops?" I asked.

He looked at me and all of a sudden his eyes turned green like a cat's at night and my knees wabbled a little.

"You wouldn't call the police, would you?" he asked.

I wiped my forehead and it was covered with sweat.

"I should say no," I said. "I wouldn't think of it."

"That's the way I figured it," he said.

"I'll buy you a glass of sherry," I said. "And, if you don't mind, I'll buy me one too. When I came home I was a little fried but now I'm cold sober and I need a drink."

I gave him a glass of sherry and he sipped it and I gulped mine and took another.

"You shouldn't swill sherry," he said. "Why don't you sip it?"

I drank half my second glass.

"On account of you lose too much by evaporation that way," I said.

I sat down and faced him. He was leaning back in the chair with his hands behind his head looking at the yellow sherry in the glass.

"All right," I said. "Out with it. What's the answer?"

"What do you mean?" he asked.

"You know what I mean," I said. "What is all this business, anyway? A gag?"

"Oh no," he said. "No gag. No gag at all."

"Then what is it?" I asked. "I meet you on the street and you say you've killed a man and for all I know you maybe did and—"

He waved his hand.

"Set your mind at rest on that point," he said. "I did kill Albert Bagley."

The way he said it made me believe at last that he really had done it.

"Why?" I asked.

"Oh, just because," he said.

"You're talking like a kid that's been asked why he batted his sister with his toy fire-engine," I said. "Because why did you kill Bagley?"

He seemed annoyed.

"Must there be a reason?" he asked.

"I should think so," I said.

"Oh, maybe I didn't like his paper," he said.

"You mean you objected to his politics?" I asked.

"I can imagine nothing more trivial," he said.

"Then what was it?" I asked. "Did you do it because he's on the side of big business against the people?"

He sipped his sherry and gazed at me.

"Why should I have cared if he was against the people?" he asked. "I'm against them too. I hate the people. Some day somebody'll figure out a way to keep their women fresh and some capitalist will finish the process of making cattle of them."

"All right," I said. "That finishes it. You're crazy, that's what. You're a maniac."

He nodded thoughtfully.

"There may be something in that," he said. "I do the most inexplicable things."

"I'll say you do," I said. "What'd you do before you got the notion of bumping off publishers?"

"I traveled," he said. "Africa, Asia, South Seas. Everywhere. The more I travel, the more I hate people."

He looked into my eyes and I shivered.

"I wish you'd keep on traveling," I said.

"I'll go presently," he said.

"Why'd you come here?" I asked.

"I'll have some more sherry if you don't mind," he said.

I got him some sherry and poured myself out a slug.

"Why did you kill Albert Bagley?" I asked.

"Let's drop that subject," he said. "It annoys me. Let us say that I didn't like the comic strips he published in the *Herald.*"

I got up and walked around the room and tried to edge toward the door and considered making a break for the telephone to call the police.

"I wouldn't if I were you," he said.

His voice was casual but his eyes were turning green again and I knew right then that I couldn't force myself to turn my back to him and go for a phone.

"Listen," I said, "tell me something. Tell me why you came here."

He sipped the last of his sherry and got up.

"You wouldn't want to know," he said.

He ran his fingers through his hair and looked at me again and nodded and walked out. I took another glass of sherry and turned the light on in the hall and went out. I went to a police station and talked to the desk sergeant.

"Listen," I said, "there's a maniac running loose in this city and you fellows better catch him before he does any more damage."

The desk sergeant sniffed the air and grinned.

"The hell there is," he said. "What damage has he done so far?"

"It isn't a gag," I said, "and I'm not drunk. He killed Albert Bagley."

The desk sergeant yawned.

"So?" he said.

"So," I said. "He did. I didn't see him do it but I was standing near the spot where it happened and when I went away he followed me and told me about it."

"That's interesting," the desk sergeant said. "Who is this guy and where do we pick him up?"

"I don't know," I said.

"Then how do we go about picking him up?" he asked.

"I don't know," I said, "but you'd better do something."

The desk sergeant put his elbows on the counter and looked at me.

"What's your name?" he asked.

"John Price," I said.

The desk sergeant wrote the name down and rattled some keys in his hand.

"All right, Johnny Price," he said. "I'll make you a proposition. I'll give you just one minute to get the hell out of here and if you don't make it, then I'll throw you in the booze cage with the rest of the souses."

"But listen," I said.

He looked at his watch and rattled the keys.

"Okay," I said. "Okay, old-timer, but remember I gave you the tip."

He rattled the keys again and I left.

5

The little old man got me down and sometimes it seemed I was going crazy and I'd just imagined him and everything else. Maybe I was drinking too much and it was catching up with me, I thought. And then I remembered the bartender and how the little old man'd frightened him too and I knew I hadn't imagined anything but that it had happened.

I worried a lot at first and then I began talking and arguing with myself and I started to calm down.

"Lots of things happen you can't explain," I told myself. "The only thing is you've never bumped into them. Well, the little old man happened and you bumped into him and you can't explain him. Nobody could explain him. But don't let him get you down. On the corners they still sell newspapers and they have movies and guys bum you for dimes and the ferryboats still get a bellyache in the fog and everything happens just like it always has happened."

And then the little old man didn't scare me so much when I thought of him. I tried to forget about him and figure maybe I'd never see him again. But I couldn't forget him and I knew I'd see him some more. In a way I wanted to see him. I wanted to see him and I knew that when I did see him I'd be afraid and kind of sick at the stomach but just the same I waited for him to pop up again.

Once when I was thinking about him it popped into my head what he'd said about eating a British colonial officer.

"By God!" I said. "I'll bet he did. I'll bet he did and I'll bet he enjoyed it."

It seemed goofy me being tangled up in a thing like that.

But that's the way it was.

6

I was driving toward Bolinas and on a steep grade my car started hitting on two or three cylinders and it puffed and wheezed and made a devil of a racket. I thought I'd burned out a bearing or something but I couldn't be sure because it had never happened to me before. I made it to a garage on top of the hill and turned off the motor and got out and looked around.

A tall young fellow was sitting in the doorway of the garage. He had on white duck trousers and a blue sweater and he was playing a harmonica. He wasn't playing it very well.

"Who runs this garage?" I asked him.

"I do," he said.

"Will you have a look at this car?" I asked. "All of a sudden it went haywire on me."

He got up and put his harmonica on the chair and walked over. Steam was shooting through the vents of the hood and the car burbled like a tea-kettle.

"It's hitting on only two cylinders," I said. "Do you think you can fix it?"

He lifted the hood and looked puzzled.

"What do you suppose is wrong with it?" he asked me.

"How in hell should I know?" I asked.

"I just asked," he said.

"Well, I haven't the slightest idea," I said. "Suppose you look into it. I've got to get back to the city."

He looked up and down the road.

"Maybe somebody will come along," he said.

"You mean you don't want to fix it?" I asked.

He shook his head.

"Oh, I want to all right," he said. "I would like to help you, in fact, but I don't know a damn thing about automobiles."

"Then what the hell you doing running a garage?" I asked.

"Well, I can pump gasoline and put in oil," he said. "When anyone has serious motor trouble I lend them the tools in there and they fix it themselves. Would you like to borrow some tools?"

"No," I said, "I wouldn't know what to do with them."

"I guess we'll have to wait for someone then," he said. "Come on and sit down for a while."

He dragged out another chair and we sat in the doorway of the garage. We could see down to where white waves were pounding against the rocks and boiling up between them.

"Remarkable view, isn't it?" he asked.

"Yes," I said, "but I'm afraid I'll get sick of it if I have to spend the rest of my days here waiting for someone to fix my car. Hell of a garageman you are."

"I'm not a garageman," he said. "I'm an artist. I bought this place because I like the view. After I bought it I found out people expected me to sell them gasoline and oil and things. I tried to discourage them. I put out signs saying I didn't want any customers but that made 'em curious and business boomed for a while."

He looked down at the water and squinted his eyes.

"When I paint that just as it should be painted," he said, "I am going to give this damned garage to the first fellow who comes along."

He got up and went to the rear of the garage and got a canvas and spread it out on the ground before me.

"That's the tenth one I did," he said. "What do you think of it?"

"I'd like to see the other nine," I said.

"I gave 'em away to customers," he said. "I take it you don't like number ten very well."

"Well," I said, "I don't know anything about art but—"

He laughed.

"You didn't have to tell me that," he said.

"Nobody knows anything about art."

"Sure," I said. "Sure, I know. Every time I meet an artist he tells me the same thing and pretty soon it gets around to where he's the only fellow knows anything about art."

He smiled. It was a pleasant smile and I liked him.

"Not me," he said.

"Well, if you don't know anything about art why did you buy a garage just to be able to paint that scene down there?" I asked.

"I didn't buy the garage," he said. "My uncle bought it for me under the impression I'd turned over a new leaf and was going to run it for profit."

I looked at the picture he'd painted and it was just a lot of colors. It didn't make sense.

"How come it's so important you paint that scene the way you think it should be painted?" I asked.

He picked up the harmonica and breathed through it.

"Last fellow I explained that to laughed at me," he said.

"I won't laugh at you," I said.

"I don't think you would," he said. "You see, it's this way. When I first stopped here and looked down at those rocks and the ocean I got a certain feeling and I knew I'd have to get it down on canvas or die in the attempt."

"The feeling?" I asked.

"Yes," he said. "It isn't the rocks and the ocean I'm trying to paint; it's the feeling they give me."

"Oh," I said.

"You look down there and you feel a certain way and you look at my painting and it doesn't mean anything to you," he said. "But if you felt the same way I do, the picture would mean something to you. It means something to me but still I'm not satisfied."

What he said didn't mean anything to me either but I didn't tell him so.

About three hours later a truck-driver stopped to get some water and we asked him to look at my car. He lifted the hood and spun the crank and said it was a gasket that'd blown out or burned out or something. He found another one in stock and in a half-hour had the car fixed for me.

I offered to pay him and he shook his head and said he'd take a cigarette. He lit the one I gave him and puffed out a cloud of smoke and looked at the artist.

"You the fellow I see out here painting sometimes?" he asked.

The artist said he was and the truck-driver asked if he could see one of the pictures. He went over and looked at the canvas spread out on the ground and then looked at the scene below. He snapped the cigarette away from him and pulled his cap over his eyes and nodded.

"Pretty good," he said. "You've got it, fella."

He got in his truck and drove away and the artist looked at me and grinned.

"You see?" he said.

"I'm beginning to get the idea," I said.

We talked for a half-hour and I asked him to look me up in San Francisco and he said he would. Then I got into my car and drove away. I hoped he would look me up. I liked him. His name was Laurence Dorgan.

7

Pete's kid was sick. He was a boy of about seven years and he had pneumonia and Pete wouldn't let them take him to a hospital. Pete was afraid of American hospitals and so was his wife. And his other kid, a girl, had died in one and they decided it was the hospital had killed her.

"They got a smell there," Pete told me. "It's a dead smell. You breathe it and you die. I know. Angelina, she died there. I know."

I never tried to argue with Peter. He was the janitor of the apartment house and he could do you a lot of favors. He could keep your plumbing in order and keep you supplied with light-globes and bring you some wine he got from his brother in Sonoma County. And he could be mean as hell and rap on your door if there was a lot of talking late at night and do other things to make you uncomfortable. If he thought hospitals killed people, it was okay with me. Anything anybody wanted to think was okay with me because for all I knew they might be right.

Pete's kid got more than sick. He got so he was dying and Pete knew it. His wife knew it too and she was crying so I could hear the sound coming up the light-well. Pete came up to get me. He knew I couldn't do anything about it. He was alone and he was afraid and he wanted me for company. His wife wasn't any company. She was alone too, but she wanted to be alone. She didn't like it that I came in.

The kid was in a little bed in the corner and he wasn't breathing regularly and when he did breathe he made a funny sound that pulled the hair on my head tight and made me want to go away. Pete explained that he hadn't called the doctor because the kid was dying and it wasn't any use putting out three dollars just to have a doctor tell you that he couldn't do anything about it.

As I say, I never argue with people because maybe they're right.

The kid moaned a little bit and tried to open his eyes, and his lips opened and he called for his mother and when she came over her crying frightened him and he wanted her to go away.

He knew he was dying too and he was afraid but he wasn't trying to run away any more because he was tired out and besides it didn't do any good.

The mother backed away and stuffed her apron into her mouth and made sounds as if she was choking and Pete put his hands in his pockets and took them out and looked at a pink and blue calendar on the wall and shook his head.

I heard a sound and I looked around and the little old man was coming in. He was walking right in as if everybody was expecting him and he was late but didn't care very much about it. He nodded to me.

"How do you do?" he said.

He walked over and looked at the kid and then looked at Pete.

"The little one is dying," he said.

Pete nodded his head and didn't say anything and his wife's eyes popped wide open and she backed away. They both took it for granted he was a friend of mine and I'd asked him to come down and they thought it was a funny thing for me to do but they didn't say anything. I realized that it didn't seem a bit queer to have the old man pop in like that and the thing that startled me was that I felt that way about it. I knew I should feel amazed or frightened but I didn't.

The little old man clasped his hands behind his back and stood with Pete and me and the four of us stood around and watched the kid die. We watched his face turn red and then white and then start to get blue. And we heard a gargling sound and saw the kid stiffen out and then go limp. We knew the second he was dead.

The mother screamed as if something horrible had just peeked through the dark bedroom at her and hid her face on the kid's chest so's she wouldn't have to see him. Pete looked at her for a minute and then turned and went into the kitchen and came back with some angelica wine and three glasses. He poured us all a drink and we drank and looked at each other and didn't say anything.

The mother prayed awhile and then got up and faced us and wrung her hands and moaned.

The little old man looked at her and then at Pete.

"It was very nice," he said. "It was very nice he could die so early."

He nodded his head and set down his glass and glanced about him and went out the door.

The mother ran over to the door and closed it and crossed herself.

"He was the devil," she said. "He had green eyes. We have sinned and he took our bambino."

She screamed and began pounding Pete on the chest.

"He was the devil, do you hear me?" she said.

Pete pushed her away and looked at the kid and me and shook his head and looked at the pink and blue calendar. Then he got annoyed at his wife's shrieking and he stomped his foot.

"Shut up, woman," he said. "God took your bambino."

8

It was a couple days later I went to my apartment and found the little old man sitting before a coal fire he'd built in my fireplace. He was sipping some of my sherry. The hair on my head got tight like it always did when I first saw him.

"How do you do?" he said.

"Fine," I said. "Like my sherry?"

He held the glass to the light and twisted it.

"Fair," he said. "Only fair."

"You tell me your favorite brand and I'll stock it," I said. "That is if you're going to insist on popping in here when I'm gone."

He shrugged.

"You never can tell," he said.

"I'm getting tired of all this," I said.

He lifted his eyebrows.

"So?" he asked.

"Yes," I said. "What's the idea, anyway?"

"No particular idea," he said.

"Who are you?" I asked.

"What you see," he said.

"I mean what's your name and what do you do?" I said.

"Oh, I use various names and do various things," he said. "None of them would interest you."

"Yes, they would," I said. "What's one thing you do, for instance?"

"Oh, I kill people," he said.

"You mean you've killed other men besides that publisher?" I asked.

"Three or four," he said.

"Name one," I said.

"Well, there was Mortimer Herrick," he said.

"Mortimer Herrick!" I said. "Why, you didn't kill him. His partner did. James Farland killed him."

"That's what the police thought," the little old man said. "The police always get things wrong."

"How'd you do it?" I asked.

"It was easy," he said. "Herrick and Farland were drinking in their hotel room and when Herrick had his back turned I walked in and picked up a revolver he'd unpacked from his bag and shot him. He was a big man and the room shook when he fell."

"It could have happened that way," I said. "Why did you do it?"

He was annoyed.

"Why?" he said. "Just because I wanted to."

"Hate him?" I asked.

"No more than anyone else," he said.

He glanced up at me and an idea came to me and I felt sweat in the palms of my hands.

"Hate me, too?" I asked.

"No more than anyone else," he said.

His lips curved a little bit and it seemed he was smiling.

"Good God!" I thought.

I thought over what he'd said and I remembered something. I took it up so's to turn the conversation away from a spot where it was making me uncomfortable and afraid.

"You didn't kill Herrick," I said. "I know you didn't because Farland swallowed poison in his cell and that proves he did it."

"All it proves was he knew he couldn't get out of the trap the police had built around him," said the little man. "He lost his courage and he swallowed cyanide."

"Papers said it was strychnine," I said.

"I should know," he said.

"Why?" I asked.

"Because I smuggled it in to him," he said.

"You're a maniac," I said.

"You said that before," he said.

"I know you are," I said. "You're just imagining things because you're crazy. You didn't kill Herrick or Bagley or any of the others. If you did, how come you haven't been caught? You're not a magician or something supernatural, are you?"

"Oh no," he said. "I'm just an ordinary man but it seems I have peculiar mental reactions."

"That wouldn't keep you from being caught if you really did kill those fellows," I said.

"The reason I'm not caught," he said, "is because I have a gift."

"A gift for what?" I asked.

"For unobtrusiveness," he said.

He got up and went to the door and turned and faced me. He looked me in the eye.

"You do believe what I have told you, don't you?" he asked.

"Yes," I said.

His lips twitched slightly.

"Afraid?" he asked.

"Afraid of what?" I asked.

"Of me, for instance," he said.

"Hell, no," I said. "Why should I be afraid of you?"

"I wouldn't know," he said.

He went out the door and I stood where I was a second and then ran to the door and looked up and down the hall and he wasn't in sight. He had a gift for unobtrusiveness all right.

9

It was late at night and I was feeling like hell and couldn't sleep and so I took a walk for myself and finally wound up in Golden Gate Park. I came to a little lake and I heard splashing and wondered what kind of fish it was making a noise like that. I walked closer and looked between the shrubbery and I saw it wasn't a fish but a girl all naked and white in the moonlight swimming around with slow, easy strokes. Once in a while she'd turn over on her back and that would make the splashing sound. The lake wasn't very deep and when she stood up the water wasn't over her thighs.

She was looking toward me and I didn't think she saw me but she did.

"Hello," she said.

I turned and I was going to run and then I thought: "What the hell, she won't hurt you."

So I turned back and said hello to her. She walked toward shore and shook her head and the moonlight shone on her wet face and she was smiling.

"What's the matter?" she asked. "Afraid of me?"

"No, lady," I said. "But I'm embarrassed as hell."

She laughed then and turned her back to me and sat down and looked across the lake.

"Come sit down," she said.

I sat down and saw that she had black hair and that her white skin wasn't a trick of the moonlight but that it really was the color of snow except where it was just a trifle pink.

She started spanking her thighs with her hands and the noise was so loud it startled me.

"It's cold," she said.

"Yes," I said, "and that just makes it all the easier to understand what you're doing swimming around here this time of night."

"Oh, I just like to swim here," she said. "It's so quiet."

"You're taking an awful chance, sister," I said.

She turned toward me.

"Why?" she asked.

"Listen, sister," I said, "it stands to reason you're dumb or you wouldn't be here the way you are. But you can't convince me you're so dumb you don't know you're taking a chance swimming around naked in a spot like this. My Lord! Most men catching you like this wouldn't waste their time just talking."

She spoke seriously.

"Wouldn't they?" she asked.

"No," I said, "and I wouldn't bet too much on myself under ordinary circumstances."

She put her hands on her breasts.

"They get cold," she said.

"Do you do this often?" I asked.

"Yes," she said. "Almost every night."

"And you've never been bothered?" I asked.

"Sometimes," she said.

I lit a cigarette and flipped the match into the water.

"Maybe I get you now," I said. "You want to be bothered, eh?"

"Oh no," she said. "I don't like it."

"What do you do then?" I asked.

"Oh, I just swim away," she said.

"And they don't hang around and wait for you to come out?" I asked.

"Yes," she said, "but I run very fast."

"You must, sister," I said.

I reached over and caught her shoulder but it was still slippery and she jerked away and dived into the water and swam out of reach. She floated on her back and looked at me. I stood up suddenly and she splashed over and swam away as fast as a startled fish. In the middle of the lake she floated again.

"Why did you do that?" she called to me.

"Just wanted to see what you'd do," I said.

"Come on back."

"Not until you go away," she said.

"I won't hurt you," I said.

"Go away," she said.

"Not until you come out," I said.

"Go away," she said.

"I'll make you come out," I said.

I really had touched her just to see what she'd do and now she was convinced I was trying to start something and I was sore because she wouldn't come out and let me prove that I didn't intend to harm her.

I got five or six rocks from the edge of the water and tossed one in. It made a splash and a wide ripple.

"Come on out or I'll throw these at you," I said.

She didn't answer, so I threw a rock and it landed near her with a loud splash. There was another splash and she disappeared under water as quickly as a seal and I saw a quick flash of her white body going under water and then I didn't see her any more. I waited and she didn't come up again and for a while I was afraid she'd drowned and then I figured she'd reached the shadows on the other side and sneaked out of the water and dressed and gone home.

So I went home, too.

10

A couple of days later Dorgan, the artist I'd met at the garage atop the hill, came to see me and he had a suitcase in his hand. He came in and dropped the suitcase and asked me did I have anything to drink and I gave him one and he sat in a chair and looked around my room.

"Your etchings aren't bad," he said, "but your water-colors are execrable. This brandy was on the vines less than a year ago."

He had a thin face, and hair that hung down over his forehead and a freckled nose and a way of grinning that made you not care very much what he said.

"What you doing here?" I asked.

"Oh, I finished the thing I was doing on the hill and I didn't have anywhere to go," he said.

"I happened to find your address in my pocket, so I came here."

"Finish your picture the way you wanted to do it?" I asked.

"Yes," he said. "God! I'm glad that's over."

"Sounds like a toothache," I said. "What'd you do with it?"

"Oh, I sent it to an exhibition," he said. "They'll probably turn it down."

"What'd you do with the garage?" I asked.

"Shipped the keys to my uncle," he said. "I'll probably never get another dime out of him."

"How about some whisky?" I said. "It's bad, too."

"I don't care," he said, "it'll be good for me. By the way, what do you do for a living?"

I poured some whisky.

"Nothing," I said.

"That's my ambition," he said. "How do you manage it?"

"My father left me some bonds," I said. "I don't get much but it's enough to live on."

"I wish I'd known you longer," he said.

"Why?" I asked.

"Because if we were old friends and you realized I was up against it you might invite me to stay here awhile," he said.

I figured I ought to get sore about him having so much brass but I wasn't.

"It's all right with me," I said. "Consider we're old friends."

He grinned and sipped his whisky and leaned back in the chair.

"We are now," he said. "What do you do with your time?"

"I just wander about and things happen to me," I said. "Usually what happens to me is getting a brick bounced off my head at some strike riot, or being on hand when a woman jumps off a ferryboat into the bay, or seeing a fire, or meeting old seamen with tall stories and unquenchable thirsts. Once in a while I get drunk and get the notion I'm tough and somebody that really is tough pops me on the jaw and I wake up in a hospital."

"That's not a bad life," he said.

"No," I said, "except for the pops on the jaw and the bricks on the head."

"They're all in the game," he said.

We had several more drinks and got pretty chummy and talkative and I told him about the little old man with the eyes that turned green when he got mad.

"I suppose you don't believe me," I said.

He grinned and the freckles on his nose skidded up and down.

"Sure I believe you," he said. "I'd believe you even if it didn't happen."

"You think I'm kidding," I said.

"No, I don't," he said. "Anything else happen to you?"

"Oh, nothing much," I said. "Only out in Golden Gate Park where people seldom go, especially at midnight, I found a lake and there was a girl swimming naked in it. I scared her and she dived under and didn't come up."

He laughed and his freckles bobbled about on his nose and he poured us a couple more drinks.

"White girl?" he asked.

"Sure," I said. "White's milk."

"Too bad she didn't come up," he said. "I'd like to have seen her."

"You may," I said. "You see, she lives at the bottom of the lake."

"Is that a fact?" he asked.

"Yep," I said. "She's a water-nymph."

"I'd like to paint her," he said.

"You'd better not try it," I said. "I won't have you painting my water-nymph so's she looks as if she'd melted and run down into her buttocks. No sale on that."

"All right," he said. "All right. I won't paint her."

11

I went to the park almost every night for a week and I prowled around as quietly as I could and didn't smoke and tried to be inconspicuous but I didn't see the girl and I decided she'd been stringing me and really didn't swim very often in the lake. Then, on the eighth or ninth night, I saw her swimming on the other side of the lake from me. She slipped through the water as smoothly as a lazy white seal and her body gleamed when she'd come out from the shadows into the moonlight.

I wanted to call to her, but I didn't because I was afraid she'd disappear and I wanted to watch her. It wasn't because she was naked. It wasn't the way she looked at all. It was because of the way she made me feel. It was a funny feeling and I couldn't describe it because I didn't understand it.

She turned on her back and her body rose and fell a little and her hair spread out on the water and if I hadn't seen her swimming just a moment before I would have thought she was a drowned woman. It was cold and I shivered dressed as I was and I wondered how she could stand it in there.

"Maybe she is a water-nymph," I thought and then I laughed and called myself a fool.

"She's just an ordinary girl with an extraordinary notion about when and where to swim," I told myself.

The girl started swimming again and she was facing me. All of a sudden she stopped and I felt as if the bushes and the trees in front of me had fallen away like a curtain and the moon was shooting all its light at me and I was as conspicuous as a giraffe. I knew she saw me.

She was quiet for a minute and then there was a splash and her white body disappeared in the water and I didn't see her any more.

I ran around to the other side of the lake and fell over rocks and bushes and bumped into trees and that's all the good it did me because she wasn't there when I arrived.

The wind was blowing pretty hard and it was getting colder and there were noises all around me and I decided I wanted to get the hell out of there. I followed a path and walked fast and the noise I heard might have been a woman's laugh and it might have been the wind or something else. Anyway I kept on going.

Dorgan guessed where I went on those nights but he didn't say anything. He'd be up when I came home and his nose would wrinkle and he'd grin at me but he wouldn't bring up the subject although I knew he was dying to.

Dorgan painted a few things and tore them up and sat around drinking my liquor in the meanwhile. He never mentioned getting himself a job and I didn't say anything about it because he was good company.

Besides that I had a feeling pretty soon there'd come a time when I'd want to talk to someone about things and I wanted that one to be the kind of a fellow who might understand and not think I was a liar or a nut.

I figured Dorgan might fill the bill.

12

When the little old man popped in quietly and unobtrusively as he usually did, Dorgan was trying to play "La Donna è Mobile" on the harmonica and he didn't pay any attention to him. The little old man nodded to me and poured himself a drink and watched Dorgan.

"Well, well," I said, "and so you're back."

The little old man glanced briefly at me and back at Dorgan.

"Yes, I'm back," he said.

"I ought to get used to it pretty soon," I said. "What have you been doing? Anything interesting or exciting?"

He didn't even look at me.

"Not particularly," he said.

He was standing in the middle of the room with his hands in his pockets looking at Dorgan. Pretty soon Dorgan glanced up at him and then at me as if to ask for an introduction or explanation.

"This is Larry Dorgan," I said, "and this is—What's your name?" I asked the little old man.

He turned his head slowly and stared at me.

"Name?" he said. "I told you I didn't have one."

Dorgan looked puzzled and then he grinned.

"Oh, this is your friend," he said.

He turned to the little old man.

"You the fellow who killed that publisher?" he asked.

The little old man nodded.

Dorgan grinned and put down the harmonica and got up and caught the little old man's hand.

"Glad to know you," he said. "I've always wanted to know a murderer."

The little old man looked into Dorgan's eyes.

"Have you?" he asked.

Dorgan looked puzzled again and stepped back.

"Well, maybe not," he said.

He got himself a drink and took his seat and crossed his long legs and stared at the little old man.

"Do you do that often?" he asked.

"What?" the little old man asked.

"I don't know exactly," said Dorgan. "But you generated a look. I'd swear your eyes changed color."

The little old man shrugged.

"That may be so," he said.

"It gave me goose bumps," said Dorgan.

"So?" said the little old man.

"Quite so," said Dorgan. "You know, I believe Price now. I really believe you killed the publisher and did those other things he says you claim you did."

There was no expression on the little old man's face.

"Your belief in my veracity is gratifying," he said. "Thanks."

"Think nothing of it," said Dorgan.

He spoke in a light tone of voice but he wasn't grinning any more. He was puzzled and impressed and interested.

"Do you kill people because you hate them or just because you get a kick out of it?" he asked.

The little old man poured himself another drink and walked around the room, looking at some of the paintings Dorgan had tacked up.

"Oh, for various reasons," he said. "This painting is excellent."

Dorgan sat up straight in his chair and spilled his drink.

"That's it," he said. "God, that's what I want to do! I want to paint you. Will you sit for me?"

"Perhaps," said the little old man. "Some time."

He gazed at Dorgan and then at me and nodded and went out the door. Dorgan sat looking at me. He was licking his lips.

"Good God!" he said. "What a subject he'd make!"

"I'll bet he would," I said. "Nice old boy, isn't he? Him slipping in like that's just about as pleasant as finding a cobra in your bed."

"Lord, but is he interesting!" said Dorgan.

"Too damned interesting," I said. "He gives me the willies. I tell you I've got to do something about that fellow, Dorgan."

"Not yet," said Dorgan. "I've got to paint him first."

"Sure," I said. "Sure, let him stick around until he takes a notion to work out on me just because you want to paint him."

"You don't really believe he's going to do anything to you, do you?" asked Dorgan.

"He might," I said.

"What?" asked Dorgan.

"I don't know," I said. "That's what gives me the willies."

"Well, what are you going to do about him?" Dorgan asked.

"I don't know that either," I said. "I've got a double dose of willies and I don't like it."

13

And so that's the way things were with me. Pestered by the little old man, trying to catch the girl in the lake, and supporting an artist who painted things and threw them away. It was all very goofy. It had never happened to me before and I don't suppose anything like it ever happened to anyone before. But that's the way it was.

It had happened to me and it was still happening.

By being extra quiet and careful I managed to see the girl swimming more often at night. Every time I saw her it did something to me. It was like being happy while I was watching her and it was like being hungry and thirsty when I wasn't. I suppose she worried me more than the little old man but for a different reason.

I'd hide behind a tree or some bushes for an hour or so and I'd hear a faint splashing and I'd see her swimming gracefully and easily. Sometimes it was moonlight and sometimes it was dark and I could barely see something white in the water. Sometimes she would swim for an hour or more and sometimes I would barely get a glimpse of her and then she would disappear.

I didn't try to catch her any more. I knew it was impossible and I thought if I behaved myself and didn't frighten her, eventually she would come out on the bank and talk to me again.

That's what I wanted. To talk to her.

One night I didn't try to hide but sat on the bank in plain sight and hoped if I remained quiet she would speak to me again. I didn't hear her or see her when she went into the water. She was in the middle of the lake, swimming slowly when I first noticed her. I felt like calling out but I didn't.

She turned toward me and her head lifted a little and I knew she saw me. I didn't move a muscle. Finally she started swimming again. First she swam away from me and then she swam back toward me. She came pretty close and I moved a little and again she reminded me of a frightened white seal the way she splashed and turned and sped away. She got to the middle of the lake and floated. Her arms were extended from her body and they rose and fell slowly with the ripples caused by her swimming.

It was so quiet I could hear my watch tick. The birds and insects and things were silent and even the wind had stopped blowing. I couldn't stand it.

"Come on over here and talk to me," I called. "I won't hurt you."

She turned over in the water and in three or four strokes she'd reached the shadows on the other side and was gone.

After that I didn't dare call to her. I would sit on the bank and she'd swim back and forth before me but never come very close to where I was sitting. Some nights she wouldn't appear at all and I would sit for hours and smoke cigarettes until I would get tired and go home. I would feel so disappointed that I wouldn't even speak to Dorgan. He'd grin at me and roll over in bed and go to sleep. He'd never mention it next morning.

I could tell he was all steamed up with curiosity but he was waiting for me to say something.

The little old man popped in on Dorgan when I was away once and when I got home Dorgan was walking up and down the room banging his fists together and swearing.

"I've got to paint that fellow even if he slits my throat the moment I'm finished," he said. "God! Do you know he sat and half-smiled at me and looked into my eyes, and my stomach just rolled over and over. I'm still sick!"

"I know how you feel," I said. "What'd he say?"

Dorgan gave me a funny look.

"Nothing," he said. "Not a damned word. He just came in and looked at me and went out."

"That's plenty," I said.

"Plenty," he said.

"We can't go out howling for the cops," I said.

"Not even if we wanted to," he said. "They wouldn't believe us. Besides how'd we lead them to the little old man?"

"I ran into that problem once," I said. "It stumped me."

He took a drink.

"Oh, well," I said, "let's forget it. After all he may be harmless."

"Sure," said Dorgan.

"It's silly to worry about him," I said.

"Sure it is," Dorgan said. "Anyway I'm not worrying about him. I'm not afraid of the little skeezix."

"Neither am I," I said.

"You're a damned liar," he said.

"You bet I am," I said.

"Me, too," he said.

14

I happened to drop into the bar where George worked and another bartender started to serve me and George butted in and poured my Scotch.

"I been wanting to see you," he said.

"What about?" I asked.

George started polishing a glass and leaned over the bar and spoke in a low voice.

"Remember that little old guy?" he asked.

"You mean the fellow who gave you a look and made you change your mind about socking him after he'd splashed beer in your face?" I asked.

"Sure," said George. "That's the guy."

"All right," I said. "What about him?"

"He's in my hair," said George. "Down my back and in my craw."

"Chiseling drinks?" I asked.

"Hell no," he said. "The old sonofagun's got plenty of money. Wish he'd spend it somewheres else."

"Well, what's the complaint?" I asked.

"Better have another drink," George said.

"Okay," I said. "Half mineral water."

George poured the drink and started wiping another glass.

"Lord a'mighty," he said. "That guy!"

"Don't be so damned mysterious," I said. "What's biting you?"

George stopped polishing the glass and beads of sweat stood out on his head as he leaned over and spoke to me.

"He comes in here and buys drinks and looks at me," he said.

"The hell he does," I said.

"Yessir," he said. "He buys drinks and *looks* at me."

"You could have him arrested for that," I said.

George didn't smile.

"Aw, quit pulling my leg," he said. "I ain't kidding. I'm up a creek, I tell ya. 'Way up."

"All right, George," I said. "I've got a notion what's biting you. It isn't a joking matter, I guess."

"I know damn well it isn't," he said. "He looks at me, you see, and his eyes grow bigger and bigger and then they grow small again and all of a sudden they turn green."

I swallowed my drink and remembered how I felt under the same circumstances and I felt sorry for George.

"Give me another," I said, "and have one yourself."

"Thanks, I will," he said.

He swallowed one straight and wiped his mouth with the bar-cloth.

"It's like I told you once," said George. "When his eyes go green on me I have the same feeling I had once when I come face to face with a rattlesnake raised up on his hind end and snapping his fangs at me."

"I know," I said. "I've had the feeling."

"And I know he's planning to do something to me and I'm afraid," said George. "But there ain't nothing I can do about it."

"Not much," I said.

"I told him to get the hell out of here once," George said, "and he give me that 'I'll-cut-your-heart-out' look and went back and talked polite and dignified as you please with the boss and I 'most got canned for being rude to a customer. You know, when he was talking to the boss you'd of swore he was a preacher."

"He *can* look harmless," I said.

"I don't know what to do," said George. "I can't go to the cops about him because he hasn't done anything to me. I'd lay for him in an alley and bang his head out of shape with a window-sash but—"

George hesitated.

"But what?" I asked.

"I'm afraid," George said. "It's like I told you; I couldn't bring myself to touch him any more than I could pet a rattlesnake on the head."

"What's he got against you?" I asked.

"I dunno," said George. "Maybe it's because I laughed at him that night and maybe it's because he don't like my looks. How the hell should I know? He's just got it in for me, that's all."

"Oh, forget it, George," I said. "Maybe it's just your imagination."

I knew it wasn't.

George glared at me.

"I hope tonight you wake up and he's in bed with you," he said.

15

I'd been waiting about an hour and it seemed the girl wasn't going to be swimming that night and I was just about to leave when I noticed her and she was swimming close to me and looking up at me.

"Hello," she said.

Her voice was the same as it had been the first night I saw her.

"Hello," I said.

She swam a few strokes and climbed out on the bank and shook herself and sat down several feet from me.

"I'm glad you came out," I said. "I wanted to talk to you."

She nodded.

"I know it," she said. "You've been waiting a long time."

"Not only tonight but a lot of nights," I said.

"I know it," she said. "I saw you every time. I laughed at you that night you fell over things and ran into a tree. Were you hurt?"

"Not much," I said. "You must be able to see in the dark."

"I can," she said. "A little."

"I wouldn't be surprised," I said. "What made you decide to come out tonight?"

"To see if you'd do what you did before," she said.

"I won't," I said. "I won't ever again."

She smiled and moved closer.

"I don't think you will," she said. "I like you."

"Do you?" I said. "Why, you don't know me at all."

She laughed and her laughter was rippling and gay.

"Oh yes I do," she said. "Oh yes I do, Johnny Price."

I dropped my cigarette.

"How did you know my name?" I asked.

"Your friend told me," she said.

"What friend?" I asked.

"The nice old man," she said.

She described the little old man to me.

"My God!" I said. "What do you know about him?"

"Not much," she said. "Except that he's nice."

I felt kind of dizzy. Here was the girl and the little old man linked together. Things were getting altogether too complicated.

"You two come from the same place?" I asked.

"Oh no," she said. "I met him only a few days ago."

I felt a little better.

"How did you happen to meet him?" I asked.

"He liked the flowers," she said. "He came by and he liked the flowers and we talked about them. Then he told me he knew about me swimming in the lake and you hiding and watching me. He didn't have to tell me that because I knew it already."

"So he's been following me out here!" I said. "My Lord!"

"Don't you like the nice old man?" she asked.

"No I don't," I said, "and the next time you see him you had better run like hell."

"He's a nice man," she said. "He liked my flowers."

"What flowers?" I asked. "Where do you come from? Where do you live?"

She waved her arm in a half-circle.

"Over there," she said. "You can't come."

"Why not?" I asked.

"You can't," she said.

"Can't I ever see you anywheres except here at night?" I asked.

She shook her head.

"No," she said. "Not ever."

I moved closer to her and it was as if I had startled some woods creature. She jumped up and stood poised on the edge of the lake. Her black hair was partly dry and it tumbled back over her shoulders and half-hid her face, which was turned toward me.

"That," I thought to myself, "is all the real beauty you've ever seen. Her standing there not ashamed of her nakedness but ready to flee if you touch it."

"Don't go," I said. "I wasn't going to touch you."

She hesitated and then came back and sat down near me.

"Don't ever do it," she said, "or I won't ever talk to you again. And I like to talk to you, Johnny Price."

"Talk to me now," I said. "Tell me about yourself. Why do you come out here at night and swim?"

She rested her chin on her knees and studied me soberly.

"Because I have to," she said.

"Why?" I asked.

She wrinkled her forehead and thought hard for the right words.

"Because ever since I was a little girl I've hated to wear clothes and to do the things other girls did," she said. "But I tried to do those things and it made me unhappy. When I come out here and swim I am not unhappy and I forget about the other things."

She was silent for a while.

"You see, I belong here," she said.

She got up and smiled at me and slipped into the water and I called to her but she didn't turn back. She slid through the water with hardly a ripple and soon she was across the lake and out of sight.

I walked through the park and it seemed I saw the little old man hiding behind every tree and I began sweating and hurried up and that made me sweat all the more.

16

Dorgan was awake that night and I was glad because I wanted to talk. He was sitting up in bed with a cigarette in one hand and a glass of brandy and seltzer in the other. There was just room in bed for his long legs.

I got myself a brandy and soda and lit a cigarette and walked back and forth and tried to think of a way to start the conversation.

He watched me awhile and the freckles skidded up and down his nose and he grinned at me.

"What's biting you?" he asked.

"Oh, nothing much," I said.

"You're a liar," he said.

"Oh well," I said, "it's this way. I've been going to the park every night watching the girl and trying to get her to talk to me again and tonight she did."

"Find out something that shattered your illusion?" he asked.

"No," I said. "I didn't find out anything. That's what's biting me. She won't tell me who she is or what she is or why she is or where she lives."

"Hm," he said. "Sort of a female little old man, eh?" he said.

"About as mysterious," I said. "Only she's beautiful—she's—"

"You're in love with her?" he asked.

"I don't know," I said. "I hadn't thought of that."

"It amounts to the same thing," he said. "You think you are. A naked woman—"

"Oh, cut it," I said. "Her nakedness doesn't count. I don't ever think of her being undressed. In fact, it'd seem strange if she wore clothes. Give me credit for not being a ten-year-old peeping Tom, will you?"

"I'm sorry," he said. "She's a vague, mysterious, illusory being and she intrigues you."

"Something like that," I said.

"But if you'd see her dressed in a pink blouse and a blue skirt behind the counter or typing letters you wouldn't look at her twice," he said.

"She isn't a clerk or a stenographer," I said.

"How in hell do you know?" he asked.

"I don't know," I admitted. "Only I can't imagine her—"

"You can't imagine her doing anything but swimming naked in a lake under the moon," he said.

"There's more than that," I said. "There's something about her. Oh hell!"

"Don't let your curiosity spoil it for you," he said. "After all, she may be a shop girl. If you mind your own business she'll always be the perfect, sexless embodiment of beauty you imagine her to be."

"I can't mind my own business," I said. "I've got to find out things."

"Sure," he said. "I know. I had to find out what made my father's watch work, too, and when I got through it was busted and I got a whaling."

"I'll take a chance," I said.

"Anyway," he said, "she'll take your mind off the little old man."

"That's just it," I said. "That's another thing that's biting me. The little old man's followed me out there."

"The hell he has," said Dorgan.

"Yes," I said, "and he's found out more about her than I have. He's found out where she lives."

Dorgan poured his drink on a small fire his cigarette had started in the bedclothing.

"Get me another, will you?" he asked. "Think there's some link between the two, the little old man and the girl?"

"I did at first but I'm sure now that she never saw him before a week or so ago," I said.

I gave him another drink.

He swallowed it and handed the glass to me for a refill.

"This is getting altogether too damned impossible," he said. "After all we're not kids. Why in hell should someone be trying to sell us a fairy tale?"

"I don't know," I said. "Maybe it isn't a fairy tale. Maybe it's something Poe didn't get around to writing and so it's happening to us."

"That damned little old man!" he said.

"I'm afraid he'll do something to her," I said.

"I hadn't thought of that," he said. "I was thinking of what he might do to me and what he's already done to me by being in existence."

"I don't want him to do anything to her," I said.

I started walking the floor again. He smoked awhile, then threw his cigarette away and got up and started walking back and forth too.

"You're out of step," he told me.

17

Dorgan and I got into the habit of dropping in and having drinks where George worked and every time we went in George was feeling worse. He was losing weight and his face was getting white all except his nose, which showed he was patronizing himself a lot.

"If he'd only say something to me," George said. "If he'd only come in with a gun and give me a chance to outrun a bullet. If only he'd do some damned thing instead of just pop in here once in a while and look at me."

"We don't enjoy his company, either," said Dorgan.

"I'm getting so I'd feel relieved if he'd pull a knife on me or chuck a bomb between me 'n' my apron," said George.

"He doesn't advertise his plans," I said.

"That's part of his peculiar charm," said Dorgan.

Dorgan felt the same way George and I did about the little old man but he still insisted he wanted to have a crack at painting him.

"Would you paint him as he is or just the way he makes you feel?" I asked.

"If I painted him the way he makes me feel," said Dorgan, "you'd think it was a photograph of him. A mild little guy who, when you look at him close, has something about him that makes your blood run cold. To paint him properly I would have to mix paint and blood and bile and ice water on my palette. But, anyway, I would like to try."

What got on all of our nerves was we didn't know where to find him nor even if he stayed in the city. It wouldn't have been so bad if he had appeared on some sort of schedule. What made it tough was the unexpected way he'd show up. We never knew if each time was the last time or whether he'd be in the next day or the next month.

One night Pete, the janitor, came in and his face was white and his black mustache was quivering at the ends. He shook his fist in my face.

"You tell 'im to stay away," he told me. "At's all. You tell 'im I no like him."

"Hold on," I said. "What's up? Tell who to stay away?"

"Thata man," said Pete. "Thata leetle ol' man who says it wasa nice my bambino she die. You tell him to stay away."

"What's he been doing?" I asked.

Pete banged his fist into the palm of his hand.

"Godadamn," he said. "What'sa she been doin'! I tell you. She . . ."

Pete used a lot of Italian to tell his story but I got the gist of it. He and his wife and their six or seven kids were sitting around the dinner table and the little old man walked in. He didn't say hello or explain why he was there. He just stood and looked at them.

Pete got up and offered him something to eat. The little old man refused. Then Pete asked him to have a chair and the little old man shook his head. Pete looked at his wife and his wife looked at him and the kids stared pop-eyed at the little old man. The youngest one rubbed her fist into her eyes and started to whimper and Pete batted her one alongside the ear. The kid bawled and this set the others off and Pete batted whatever kids he could reach. He wasn't sore at them. His nerves were on edge.

The little old man went into the kitchen and poured himself some angelica. He told Pete it was good wine. Pete offered him a bottle of it and he shook his head.

Then Pete got up courage and asked him what he wanted.

The little old man sipped his angelica.

"In Italy," he said, "they have the maffia and frequently when the black wind has extinguished the moon and the darkness is so heavy that it muffles the assassin's footsteps there is a sharp cry in the night."

He set his empty glass on the table and stared at Pete.

"And in the morning," he said, "the villagers gather around a corpse and cross themselves."

Pete tried to say something but he was too frightened to make a sound.

"The Italians are a race after my own heart," said the old man.

From then on Pete included more and more Italian in his story and it wasn't so easy to make out. I gathered, however, that he took the little old man to be some kind of a Black-Hander and suspected me of being in on the plot. I did what I could to cheer him up but I didn't have much success.

Pete went out shaking his head and muttering to himself.

When Mrs. Pete saw me she glared at me and sailed past without speaking.

I didn't get any more good wine from Pete's brother in Sonoma.

18

Dorgan had a picture in an exhibition at the Palace of Fine Arts and some Western art association was going to give a cash prize for the best entry. Dorgan's picture was of a Japanese girl and I liked it. Dorgan liked it, too.

"It's a Japanese Mona Lisa," he told me.

"You'd better tell the judges about that," I told him.

"It wouldn't do any good," said Dorgan. "If the original Mona Lisa were hung in that exhibition the judges'd condemn it on the grounds it's too sentimental or something."

"What's your reason for entering your painting, then?" I asked.

"Oh," he said, "it's a gamble like putting a nickel in a slot machine. Maybe the judges'll get me mixed up with the artist they intend to give the prize to."

"Do they make up their minds ahead of time?" I asked.

"Usually," he said. "You see they almost invariably ask some prominent and well-publicized artist to exhibit in order to attract attention. Naturally it'd be an insult to him if they didn't give him the prize."

"That's why you don't think you'll win the prize, eh?" I said.

"Yes," he said.

"The fox didn't decide the grapes were sour until after he'd lost the high jump," I said.

"You go to hell," he said.

We went to the exhibit and a lot of the stuff looked like the paintings they hang in the high class restaurants. Mostly it was trees and ocean views and hills.

"If they didn't have cypress at Carmel most California artists would starve to death," said Dorgan.

"No they wouldn't," I said. "They could keep on painting Fisherman's Wharf."

"You're right," said Dorgan. "Look. Here's the painting that'll win the prize."

The painting was of a tree on a rock. It was a sway-backed tree with a top something like half a cantaloupe.

"That seems familiar," I said.

Dorgan bowed to the picture.

"Only God can make a tree," he said.

"He must have left the Carmel cypress to an assistant," I said.

We went on around the gallery and Dorgan didn't like most of the paintings and those he did like he liked only a little bit. He said he wasn't jealous or anything but honest and he didn't give a damn for anyone who wasn't.

Dorgan didn't win the prize. The fellow who painted the cypress did.

After the judging there was a commotion in front of the prize-winning picture and Dorgan and I squeezed into the crowd and we saw the canvas had been ripped to ribbons.

Dorgan was feeling pretty good when we went out.

"I could love the fellow who did that," he said. "He's a real art critic. Now if he'd only dynamite the Coit Tower—"

His jaw dropped and his eyes bugged out and he caught my arm with one hand and pointed with the other. I didn't see anything.

"What the hell?" I asked.

"He just ducked around the corner," said Dorgan.

"Who?" I asked.

"The little old man," said Dorgan.

19

After that Dorgan went back to painting pictures and destroying them as soon as he finished them. He was going to destroy the picture of the Japanese girl but I wouldn't let him. I wanted it myself. He wasn't painting very often. He was too busy worrying about the little old man and wanting to paint him.

"I don't really want to," he told me. "I have to, that's all."

We got on some pretty good binges because both our nerves were on edge. We didn't stage the brannigans at the bar where George worked any more. George was so miserable all you could do drinking his liquor was get on a crying jag. The last place he had seen the little old man was in a public lavatory.

"You can't tell me," he said. "That's where he hides. In one of them bowls."

I kept going out to the park at night. Dorgan wanted to come along and I wouldn't let him. He didn't insist.

"I'm a pretty good judge of character," he said, "and if I saw her and told you what I thought she was you'd get sore and I'd have to go find myself another home."

20

It was a warm night and you could smell the trees and flowers, and the moon was out just enough so's to change the park and make you think it was some place you'd never been before. The girl was sitting on the bank when I came up and she smiled at me as I sat beside her.

"I don't like you doing this," I said. "I know hardly anyone ever comes around here, but you're taking a chance just the same. You didn't even look around when I came up. What if I had been someone else?"

"How could you be?" she asked.

"I mean what if a stranger had come up behind you?" I asked.

"I wouldn't have stayed," she said. "I knew it was you."

She was looking at me, and the moonlight was in her eyes, and her teeth showed just a little in a smile. Her hair was loose around her shoulders and the breeze blew the scent of it to me.

"What's your name?" I asked.

"Trelia," she said.

Always before she had refused to tell me her name. I was as delighted as if she had leaned over and kissed me. I felt she was beginning to like me and that pretty soon I would find out more about her.

"Of course," I said. "Trelia. It couldn't be anything else. Tell me, where do you live, Trelia?"

I held my breath.

"After all this time," I thought, "she's going to answer your questions."

She smiled and waved her hand in a half-circle.

"Over there," she said.

"Listen, Trelia," I said. "This can't go on, you know."

"What can't?" she asked.

"You being so mysterious," I said. "I've got to know more about you. I've got to see you some place else except here."

She shook her head.

"You wouldn't like me," she said.

"Yes I would," I said.

"I wouldn't like you," she said.

She put her hands in back of her and leaned back and looked up at the moon, and it seemed the yellow rays were pouring down on her like rain.

"You're thinking she's naked," I told myself. "And you've got to cut it out."

I looked away and lit a cigarette and smoked and tried to watch the smoke blow out over the lake.

"Why wouldn't you like me?" I asked.

"I don't know," she said.

"Then why do you say it?" I asked.

"I feel it," she said. "I can't explain."

"Why shouldn't you think about her being naked?" I thought. "After all, she is."

But when I let myself think of it I felt ashamed and I couldn't figure out why. I tried to look away from her but I couldn't. It was the first time I'd been that way with her. Maybe it was the night and maybe it was the fact she'd told me her name and I felt more intimate with her.

"Have you seen the little old man any more?" I asked.

"Once," she said. "He stood back in the shadows and watched me for a while. Then he went away. He's a nice man. He liked the flowers."

"What flowers?" I asked.

"My flowers," she said.

"Where?" I asked.

She waved her hand in a half-circle.

"Over there," she said.

"You don't mind the little old man knowing where you live," I said. "Why should you mind me knowing?"

She looked thoughtful.

"He's an old man," she said. "I like old men. But not young men."

She was afraid she'd hurt my feelings.

"I like you, though," she said. "Here."

I tried to keep the conversation going but she didn't pay much attention to me. She looked out across the lake and her eyes were half-closed and she was humming to herself. After a while she turned toward me.

"This is my lake," she said. "It belongs to me. I don't want anyone else swimming in it but just me."

"I'm afraid no one else would see it that way," I said.

"And this is my park," she said. "All of it. The deer and the bears and the squirrels and the birds. I don't want anyone to bother the deer or the bears or the squirrels or the birds. They're mine and I want to feed them and play with them. I want to let them out of their cages so they can wander about in my park. The flowers are mine, too, and I don't want anyone picking them."

I couldn't figure out what'd caused her mood nor what to say about it, so I kept still.

"The seals are mine too," she said, "and I don't want people standing around laughing at them when they swim. They're beautiful and when people laugh at them I want to throw rocks at them. I did once. I threw a rock and it hit a fat man and he turned and slapped a little freckled-faced boy and the boy cried. I didn't feel sorry for the boy because he had been laughing at the seals too."

I leaned over toward her.

"Trelia," I said, "do you like me a little bit?"

She considered the matter for a while.

"Yes," she said.

I got up and looked down at her.

"Trelia," I said, "all the time you've been talking I've been wanting to kiss you."

She looked puzzled.

"Why should you want to kiss me?" she asked.

"Maybe you'll find out if you kiss me," I said.

She got up and faced me and she was undecided about what to do.

"I won't hurt you," I said. "I won't touch you. I just want to kiss you."

She stepped closer and her face was close to mine and her lips were parted and I could smell her hair and feel her body almost touching mine and I thought: "When I kiss her it'll be the only real thrill I'll ever have in my life."

And I kissed her and her lips were cold and unresponsive and it was like kissing a child.

She looked puzzled. She touched her own lips and then she reached up and touched mine. She looked at me a second and then dived into the lake and swam under water a ways, then came up and continued on across without stopping or looking back.

"I know now why I feel ashamed when I think of her being naked," I said. "I know now. It's because she's naked like a child. She's a woman and her breasts are woman's breasts and her body is a woman's body but just the same she's naked like a child."

21

The next time the little old man walked in on Pete, Pete was ready for him. Pete had been brooding over the thing and he had decided what to do. The little old man was a Black-Hander, all right, Pete figured, and he was going to come around pretty soon and ask for money. Well, Pete wasn't going to give him any. Pete had worked hard for his money.

Pete knew it didn't do any good to give money to a Black-Hander. They always came back for more and when there was no more they slit your throat or drove a knife into your back. The only way to deal with Black-Handers was to play their own game. Kill them first. If they had friends and the friends came around for revenge, kill them too. Keep this up until all the Black-Handers were dead or until they got you. That was much better than putting out money and then getting your throat slit anyway.

So when the little old man came walking in that night Pete's wife gathered up the kids and they streaked for the bedroom so's not to be in the way when Pete swung into action. Pete was a husky man and his wife had no doubt but what he could kill the little old man. The only thing that bothered Pete's wife was what the priest would think of this business of killing people. She didn't think the priest would say much, though, seeing it was a Black-Hander Pete'd killed.

Of course the police might come in but then Pete's wife figured she could explain the thing to the priest and he would tell the police to mind their own business.

The kids began to whimper and she hissed Italian curses at them and they shut up. She knelt at her bed and crossed herself and lifted her face to the ceiling and the harsh lines softened and she smiled sweetly as she prayed that Pete would be able to cut the little old man's throat without too much trouble.

Pete turned to the little old man and stared at him. He didn't plan on starting his knife work until it was necessary. He stared at the little old man and the little old man stared back and pretty soon Pete grew uneasy and his eyes dropped.

"What you want this time?" he asked.

"Oh, nothing," said the little old man. "Nothing at all."

"Why you come here?" Pete asked. "Why you all a time come here and look at me? I no like it. Godadamn! I no like it."

The little old man looked at him curiously. "So?" he asked.

Sweat began to stand out on Pete's forehead and he felt himself growing afraid. So he began to talk loudly to make the little old man think he was brave.

"You git," he said. "You git a hell out."

He took a step toward the little old man and the little old man looked into his eyes and Pete fell back and cursed in Italian. The little old man sat down and crossed his legs and looked at Pete.

Pete decided that maybe the Black-Hander wouldn't want too much money after all and it might be better to drive a bargain.

"How much you want?" he asked.

"You mean money?" asked the little old man.

"Yes," said Pete. "How much da mon?"

"Oh, I have plenty of money," said the little old man, "I don't want any."

He looked at Pete and he grew thoughtful.

"You Italians bleed an awful lot," he said. "Your veins are full of blood."

Pete shrugged his shoulders. All right, he thought, this guy was going to try to scare him into paying a lot of money and he didn't have a lot of money and that would mean somebody was going to get killed. Pete was afraid but he knew he was in for it and he acted deliberately and calmly.

He went to the kitchen table and pulled out a drawer and got a knife and a whetstone. He came out and stood in front of the little old man and spat on the whetstone and began to sharpen the knife. All the while he looked at the little old man.

Pete was praying his bluff would work and the little old man would get frightened and run away. Pete knew he would come back but he was hoping the next time he'd have more courage. Pete hadn't had much red wine that night, only five or six glasses. He decided he'd drink a lot every night after that so's he would have plenty of courage when the little old man came back.

The little old man watched Pete sharpen the knife and his expression didn't change. Pete tested the blade on his thumb several times and finally he cut himself and swore and stuck his thumb in his mouth.

The little old man smiled and Pete lost his temper. He threw the whetstone at the little old man and lifted the knife and went at him but the little old man slipped out of the chair and stepped behind it and looked at Pete. He caught Pete's eye and half-smiled and then his eyes started to grow wider and they got green and Pete crossed himself and backed against the bedroom door. The little old man stepped toward him and Pete turned and tore at the doorknob and howled for his wife to let him into the bedroom.

The little old man walked over and picked up the knife and tested its blade. Then he threw it so's it stuck into the wall. He watched it quivering there for a second, turned and glanced calmly at Pete and then went out the door.

Pete's wife opened the door and asked if he'd killed the little old man and when she saw he hadn't and that he was scared stiff she started to pull her hair and cry. The men from her village, she said, were real men, not men with water in their veins.

Pete stood it for a while and then he opened up his big hand and slapped his wife on the face. The blow sent her spinning across the room and she fell in a corner and felt her cheek and spat at him. Pete walked over and skidded his foot across the floor and kicked her on the rump where she was sitting and she screamed and went for the knife. He took it away from her and slashed her cheeks and she got another knife and it looked like there'd be hell to pay but the police came and took Pete and his wife to jail. They let them go in the morning.

Pete's wife went to the priest later that day. She told him the cut on her cheek was caused by a fall into the cellar. What she complained about and wanted the priest to speak to Pete about was the kick in the rump.

22

Dorgan was pretty tight; he was waving his glass and speaking solemnly.

"The meeting," he said, "must come to order. If the president of the First National Bank will please cease chewing gum and if Sister Abernathy will kindly quit scratching herself we will get at the business of the evening."

"Sister Abernathy has hives," I said.

Dorgan stared disapprovingly into a corner where there was nothing but a chair and frowned at Sister Abernathy.

"This," he said, "is no time to have hives. Hives are for winter when the nights are long and one is hard put to entertain oneself. I advise you, Sister Abernathy, to get yourself married to a man who also has hives and then you can spend the time scratching one another."

"What's the business of the evening?" I asked.

Dorgan brushed back his hair and drew a deep breath.

"In this city of fog and fish and shrimp and Chinamen," he said, "there dwells a sinister person who by some inward alchemistry has succeeded in changing himself from a human being to a monster. He has formed a merger with the forces of darkness and evil and death. He stalks through the streets seeking prey and none is safe from him. I propose, ladies and gentlemen, that we organize ourselves and destroy him."

I'd just as soon Dorgan's jag had taken a different turn but I tried to play in with him.

"Okay," I said, "you can count on me and fifteen sturdy slingshotmen. Where does this monster live?"

"That," said Dorgan, "is the rub. No one knows. I suspect that he inhabits an attic where spiders spin black webs and white mice with red eyes are killed and eaten by grey rats. But this may not be so. He may inhabit a cave and green, slimy, crawling things may be his companions."

"I don't like snakes," I said.

"We must find him and exterminate him," said Dorgan. "Are we coolies that we should permit him to prey upon us? Are we not American citizens? Yes? Then we must strike. No longer shall we sit around on our dorsal fins waiting for him to come to us. We must track him to his lair and crush him."

"How shall we go about killing him?" I asked.

"I don't know," said Dorgan. "Perhaps we must mold a golden bullet. Or it may be that we must concoct a rare and deadly poison. On the other hand a cord woven from the silken hair of an unkissed maiden will do the work. In any event he must die."

Dorgan paused and weaved and spilled his liquor and frowned into the corner where he'd decided Sister Abernathy was sitting.

"If the lady does not come to order," he said, "we'll call in the person of whom we were speaking and have him do her scratching for her."

He turned back to me and pointed his finger at me.

"Why do *you* sit there with your teeth in your mouth and your hands in your pocket and say nothing?" he asked. "Dolt, donkey, and dotard! Speak up!"

"I move that the meeting adjourn," I said.

"Over my dead body," he said. "Stark terror grips the land! Death in a new and malignant form lurks in every corner. A ravening wolf of destruction gnaws at the throat of civilization itself. This meeting must not adjourn until definite action has been decided upon; until we have embarked upon a campaign which shall not end until this monster lies squirming in his own gore."

"Oh, shut up, Dorgan," I said. "You're getting on my nerves."

Dorgan blinked and looked around him.

"I'm getting on my own nerves," he said. "Let's get ourselves fried in the deep grease of Steve's Martinis."

"You're already fried," I said.

Dorgan took another drink and then gazed sternly at the corner.

"*Sister* Abernathy," he said.

23

Trelia got more and more used to me and seeing's I didn't try to kiss her any more she finally got so she liked me a lot. I mean she liked me as a child would, not as a woman. I couldn't figure out if that's the way I felt about her or not. I know I didn't want to kiss her any more. What I wanted, I guess, was for her to want to be kissed—as a woman.

Dorgan was after me to bring her to the apartment to pose for him and I tried to sell her the idea. At first she wouldn't listen but I kept insisting and telling her how beautiful Dorgan would make her look and finally she began to think it over. I was afraid Dorgan wouldn't make her look beautiful but I figured if I could get her away from the park and see her in different surroundings I might understand her better. I had a notion she'd be a different person when she came to my apartment.

Finally she agreed to come but she insisted that it be late at night and made me promise to let her find her way to the apartment alone and not try to spy on her.

Dorgan was all excited. He arranged the lights and his painting things and chewed a brush as he waited for her to show up.

"Think she'll come?" he asked.

"I'm afraid she will," I said.

"What do you mean, you're afraid she will?" he asked.

"Well, I've been thinking it over," I said, "and now I'm not so damned anxious to have her come here. She'll be dressed, of course, and I'm afraid the clothes will spoil her. I'm afraid she'll be just an ordinary girl."

"Afraid of being disillusioned, eh?" said Dorgan.

"Yes," I said, "it's like you say. She might be a stenographer or a five-and-dime clerk or something. What I'm worried about is she might look like one. I wish I hadn't asked her to come."

I really wanted her to come but, as I say, I was growing afraid it might spoil things for me. I would have been disappointed if she hadn't showed up and still I was half-hoping she wouldn't.

"I'm all set to be disillusioned," said Dorgan. "The way I figure it is you've let moonlight and strange surroundings fool you. But I'm an optimistic cuss and if she's anything like you say she is, I'll have my masterpiece."

"If she does come and you paint her like you've painted things," I said, "I'll murder you. No impressionistic monkeyshines."

"Okay," he said. "No impressionistic monkeyshines."

"I told her you'd paint a beautiful picture of her," I said.

"I'll try," he said. "Of course, I can't guarantee anything. If she impresses me a certain way, then I'll have to paint her that way."

"If she doesn't impress you, I will," I said. "With a bottle."

We waited a long time and it got late and we were ready to give up and turn in when there was a soft knock on the door and I opened it and she came in. She was dressed in something green and soft and she didn't wear a hat and her hair tumbled over her shoulders. I wasn't disappointed a bit. The green thing made her look as if she were dressed in part of the lake. It was the first time I'd ever seen her in a good light and I saw she was just as beautiful as I'd imagined. Her eyes were large and round and soft and her lips were red and full and her cheeks were pink and her skin was white.

She looked up at me and her eyes were frightened. She crouched back against the door and looked around the room and back at me and it seemed as if she was ready to turn around and run away again.

"I'm glad you came," I said.

"I don't like it here," she said. "I'm going back."

"You can't," said Dorgan. "I'm going to paint you. I've got to paint you."

She looked at Dorgan and tried to make up her mind whether or not to be afraid of him.

"You're beautiful," said Dorgan. "You're the most beautiful person I've ever seen."

She smiled a little and blushed and waited for us to tell her what next to do.

"Before you start," said Dorgan, "how about a glass of wine?"

"I've never tasted it," she said, "but I'd like to try."

Dorgan had started for the kitchen. He stopped and looked back over his shoulder.

"That the truth?" he asked. "You've never tasted wine?"

"No, I haven't," she said.

"Doesn't sound reasonable," said Dorgan.

He got her a glass of wine and she looked at it and smelled it and finally tasted it. She made a face and handed him the glass.

"I don't like it," she said.

I noticed that she didn't have any paint on her cheeks or lips and no powder on her skin and she was so beautiful just looking at her made me dizzy.

"She's not a disappointment," I said to myself. "Clothes don't spoil her at all and she's just as beautiful here as she is at the lake."

But while I was drinking this I knew that something was wrong. There was something about her didn't go with her beauty. Something in the way she talked and looked around her and made me feel.

"When she's naked," I told myself, "she's naked like a child and when she's dressed the same thing's the matter."

Dorgan posed her in a chair and mixed his paints and made a sketch and finally picked up his brushes. She was still frightened and she kept looking around her and it annoyed him.

"Keep your eyes fixed on that floor lamp over there," he said. "I'm not taking a motion picture of you."

She started to get up but I motioned to her and she settled back into the chair and looked at the floor lamp. Dorgan painted awhile. Then he stared at her and started in again.

"Are you moving?" he asked.

"No," she said.

"Are you changing your expression?" he asked.

"No," she said.

"Something's wrong," he said.

Dorgan frowned and began to paint. He'd look up once in a while and study her and then go back to work.

"She's afraid of this place," I thought, "not because of anything in it but because she doesn't like being indoors. She feels trapped."

I tried to talk to her but she wouldn't say anything much. When she did talk she had trouble with her words. It wasn't like when she got started at the lake and rattled on for an hour or so telling me about her animals in the park. Finally Dorgan told me to shut my mouth on account of it was interfering with his painting.

He worked for two hours and by that time all he had on the canvas was a lot of different-colored blobs of paint. He was sweating and he was biting his lips and painting as if it were as hard as chopping wood.

He put down his brush finally and shrugged his shoulders and sat down.

"I can't do it," he said. "Not tonight. I can't get it the way it should be. Will you come back next week?"

She got up from the chair and looked at me and at Dorgan and around the room.

"I don't think so," she said.

Dorgan started to argue with her. She saw a picture of a lake hanging on the wall and went over to it.

"Did you paint this?" she asked.

"Yes," said Dorgan.

She gazed at it for a long time.

"Can you make me look as beautiful as this?" she asked.

"Even more beautiful," said Dorgan.

"Then I'll come," she said.

She wouldn't let me go home with her. When I insisted she became frightened and I was afraid she wouldn't come back, so I let her go. She smiled at me and slipped out the door and I watched her go down the hall and it seemed she was floating instead of walking. When I turned and looked around the room it was all wrong because she wasn't there.

Dorgan was pacing back and forth gnawing on a paint-brush handle.

"Damn it," he said. "I can't get it."

"What's wrong?" I asked.

"There's something missing," said Dorgan.

"There's something I try to get and it isn't there."

"I think I know what you mean," I said.

"I could paint her as she is but it would be flat and it wouldn't mean anything," said Dorgan. "Maybe I can get it tomorrow night."

"Were you disillusioned?" I asked.

"No," he said. "No, by God, I wasn't. She's the most strangely beautiful thing I've ever seen."

He spat out some splinters from the paintbrush he'd been chewing.

"I've got to get her right," he said.

He glared at me as if I were responsible for what was wrong.

"Do you know," he said, "you look at her awhile and it comes over you that maybe she doesn't breathe and eat and exist like ordinary people."

"I know what you mean," I said.

24

George, the bartender, was an Irishman and his wife was an Irishwoman and the three kids were freckle-faced and red-haired. They lived in a small house out near San Bruno and every year George went out and hauled the junk out of the yard and started a cabbage patch and the kids ran over it and stomped it out before it had a chance to grow or the neighbor's goat ate up the young shoots and George never did raise a head of cabbage. He was always trying, though.

George told his wife how the little old man was bothering him and she sniffed and said it was the whisky he was drinking that gave him such silly notions. She said she knew he was a good-for-nothing stew-bum but she hadn't realized that the booze was softening his brain until then, and she threatened to tell Father Donavan about it. George said if she did he would fix her so's she couldn't get around to mass for a month.

They bickered a lot about the little old man and then one night he showed up. The three boys had left the table early to join their gang and have a rock fight with the Italian kids from the next block and George and his wife were sopping up the last of the gravy with their bread when he came in. He walked in without knocking like he always did and stared at them without saying a word.

George swore under his breath and waved a piece of bread at him and looked at his wife and swallowed something crosswise and coughed and choked.

George's wife didn't get what George meant and she looked at the little old man.

"What do you want?" she asked. "You one of George's drunken friends?"

The little old man smiled mildly and shook his head.

"Oh, I seldom drink," he said, "and I never get drunk."

"Then you aren't a friend of George's," she said. "And what is it you want?"

"Oh, I just dropped in," said the little old man. "I just dropped in for a moment."

George's wife couldn't figure out what it was all about but he was a harmless-looking old man and she was polite after her fashion.

"Take a load off your feet, then," she said. "Sit down there and will you have a cup of tea?"

"Oh no," said the little old man, "I never drink with people who—"

He stopped and gazed vacantly around him.

George was scared but the fact he was in his own home and had his wife to back him up gave him Dutch courage.

"You mean you don't drink with people you pester and browbeat and bully and threaten," he said.

The little old man looked as if his feelings'd been hurt.

"Have I ever pestered or browbeaten or threatened you?" he asked.

"You have," said George, "and I'm not going to stand for it a minute longer. Take your ugly little mug out of my home and don't you ever shove it into the saloon again or else I'll smash it flat like a tomato that's been stepped on by a truck."

George's wife still didn't realize who the little old man was.

"Shut your ugly mouth, you cowardly brute," she told George, "or else I'll shut it for you. That's a fine way to be talking to an old man, isn't it? Do you mean to say this little fellow has been bullying and threatening you? Faugh! What a man it is I married!"

"You married a better man than your mother did," said George.

He turned to the little old man.

"It's bad enough for you to pester me at my work," he said, "but, by God, it's a damn outrage I won't stand for you to shove your monkey's mug into my own home in front of my wife. Now you get out."

The little old man leaned back in his chair and squinted his eyes at George.

"The Irish," he said, "are a race given a great deal to talk and for that they would be wiped off the earth were it not for their propensity to hate and kill one another. This pleases whatever gods there be and they leave the Irish alone for the fun they afford."

This didn't set so well with George's wife.

"I'll have you know I came from County Cork," she said, "and no wizened little goat of a man can make fun of my family."

The little old man looked mildly at her.

"The Irish are given to sudden and violent bloodshed," he said, "and he who helps bash the skull of Terry O'Shea the next day may have his skull bashed by the man for whose sake he bashed the skull of Terry O'Shea. The Irish are a strange and inexplicable and violent race and it is well they are allowed to survive, for when they are gone there will be no more interesting fools, no more colorful knaves, no more men to wage bloody battle for want of ability to take a joke."

George turned to his wife.

"Now you see," he said. "Now you see what I've been talking about."

"Now I see nothing but an insulting little blabber-mouth," she said, "and I will have none of him."

She got up and doubled up a fist as large and red as a newly-skinned ham and went for the little old man. The little old man stood up and the mildness dropped from him and his eyes grew large and started to turn green and they darted flashes of light at George's wife.

George's wife took a step toward him and the little old man coiled up like a snake and when he spoke he hissed and George afterwards swore a forked tongue came out of his mouth.

"You sit down," he said.

George's wife let her hand fall to her side and she backed up and stumbled against a chair and sat down in it and her eyes got big as overcoat buttons.

"George," she said, "George, if you're half a man you'll throw this fellow out."

George was used to doing what his wife said and he got up and faced the little old man and started to say something. But the sight of the little old man made him swallow quickly and what he swallowed choked him and he couldn't speak nor move.

His wife yelled at him to do something and George looked dumbly at her and then back at the little old man but he couldn't move a muscle.

The little old man got up and stretched and yawned and went to the table and poured himself a cup of tea and drank it. And George and his wife watched him and said nothing. The little old man walked toward the door and faced them and smiled an evil smile and bowed.

"But the Italians are just as bad," he said.

He went out and it was a full ten minutes before George's wife got calm enough to tell George he was a whisky-swilling second-cousin of a diseased pig. George hadn't even recovered enough to smack her.

25

"We must be intelligent about the matter even if it is altogether Goddamned silly," said Dorgan. "We are adults and we are supposed to have adult brains and we know ogres and ghosts and zombies do not exist. Therefore your little old man is made of flesh and blood and possesses no magic."

"Sure," I said, "that's what my intelligence tells me. It tells me that much and past that point it has nothing to say. Maybe you know the way from there on."

"No I don't," said Dorgan. "Past that point I get lost, too, but I am not headed in the direction of the supernatural. This, Johnny, is the year 1934 in the city of San Francisco and, to prove that human elements are in control, there is a general strike and policemen are beating workingmen over the heads with sticks loaded with lead."

"And the little old man slips in and out of everything and throws the fear of the devil into you and me and George and Pete and none of us know what the hell it's all about," I said. "What's your idea of the lad?"

"Well," said Dorgan, "I figure he is an ordinary human being with an enormous capacity for evil."

"That's right," I said.

"Somehow," said Dorgan, "his brain has been thrown out of gear and off its trolley and his mental processes are beyond our understanding."

"Pretty soon you'll have the whole thing solved," I said.

"His brain," said Dorgan, "is vaguely akin to that of an Edison or a Marconi."

"The hell you say," I said.

"I do say it," said Dorgan. "There is no electric light, people *know* there can be no such thing, and the brain of Edison gives us the electric light. There is no wireless and there can be no wireless and the brain of Marconi gives us the wireless."

"So what?" I asked.

"So," said Dorgan, "there is no little old man, there is no human being who can do the things the little old man does, and the brain of the little old man gives himself to us. Do you follow me?"

"I'm in the same circle," I said, "only I'm a lap ahead of you and going in the other direction. What does the brain of Mr. Dorgan give us on Trelia?"

Dorgan looked drunk and thoughtful at the same time.

"Trelia," he said, "is an altogether different kettle of fish. She eludes me."

"Me too," I said.

"Trelia," he said, "is something that should be but isn't quite. Understand?"

"The dogs," I said, "should always follow the rabbit and not cut across lots."

"Trelia," he said, "lacks but one ingredient to make her something that couldn't possibly be. With that missing ingredient I could paint her and my fame would go down the ages as an artistic and exquisite liar with paint and brush. As it is, I could paint her and everyone would know the picture was wrong but none would know why."

He got himself a drink and waved the glass at me.

"When she comes tomorrow," he said, "I'm going to find that missing ingredient and put it in the picture even though she may still lack it."

"Dorgan," I said, "you're talking phone numbers."

"Johnny," he said, "for two cents I would get fried."

26

Trelia was still dressed in the soft green dress when she came to us the next night and she was still frightened and she still seemed out of place in my apartment. Dorgan was burning to get to work on the painting and he didn't give me any time to talk to her. I don't suppose it would have done much good anyway because she seemed tongue-tied the minute she got into the apartment.

I had met her at the lake one night that week and she had crawled dripping onto the bank beside me and talked glibly about the apartment and Dorgan and the picture hung on the wall.

"It made me feel so peaceful and beautiful inside," she said; "it isn't like my lake but it makes me feel like my lake does. Do you think he can make me look like that?"

"You can't ever tell how Dorgan'll make you look," I said, "but I don't think he'll make you look like a lake of water."

"I didn't mean that," she said. "I meant something else. I think he would understand."

"I don't know whether or not I understand," I said, "but I have a feeling that might be somewheres in the neighborhood. Let me stroke your hair, Trelia."

And she moved closer and I stroked her hair and had a feeling inside that was like being homesick. That's the nearest I can get to the feeling she gave me, homesickness.

She gave me the same feeling this night only it was worse because she wasn't talking to me alone on the shores of the lake with the trees bending and making soft noises over our heads. She looked out of place in the apartment yet I thought she belonged there. I thought that and I knew I couldn't keep her there.

Dorgan worked hard that night. He painted until he perspired and all the while he swore under his breath and bit his lip and frowned.

"I can't do it," he said. "Something's wrong, maybe it's the dress."

"The dress?" she said. "I'll take it off."

She rose and held her arms over her head and inched the dress up and pretty soon it was on the floor and a white underthing was lying beside it. She was naked except for her shoes and stockings. She wasn't a bit embarrassed, no more embarrassed than she was with me at night by the lake.

"Take the shoes and stockings off, too," said Dorgan. "Maybe we'll begin to get somewhere."

She took off her shoes and stockings and sat down again.

Dorgan wasn't painting her body at all. He was just painting her head. Just the same I had a hazy idea of why he figured he might do a better job if she took off her clothes.

Dorgan got to work again and the blob of paint on the canvas started to take form and look a little bit like Trelia's face. Dorgan was working fast but he made a lot of motions before even a small spot began to look like a part of Trelia's face. At first he worked smoothly and it seemed he was getting somewheres. Then he started to study her and to frown and finally the sweat was standing out on his forehead again.

"Trelia," he said, "what are you doing?"

She looked surprised and frightened.

"Nothing," she said.

"Well then, do something," said Dorgan. "Think of something. Goddamnit! I can't get you."

She looked at me and her lips trembled and I thought she was going to cry or else run away.

"It's all right, Trelia," I said. "He didn't mean to be unkind. He's just trying to make you beautiful like the lake."

She looked doubtful but she resumed her pose and Dorgan started painting again. He painted for an hour and finally he threw his brush to the floor.

"I can't do it," he said. "I can't find the ingredient."

She stayed in the chair and looked from Dorgan to me and tried to decide what to do next.

"Get dressed," said Dorgan. "I'm through. I'm licked."

She got dressed and looked at the picture and seemed disappointed. I tried to make her stay a little longer but she wouldn't. She made me promise not to follow her and then she slipped out into the hall and went softly down it and was gone.

"What the hell's the matter?" I asked Dorgan.

He was stretched out on the bed and he was tired all over.

"How in hell do I know?" he yelled at me.

I looked at what he'd done.

"Looks like a good start to me," I said; "why didn't you go on?"

Dorgan got up and went into the kitchen and got a knife and came out and cut the canvas into ribbons.

27

And so next Dorgan started painting the little old man. He'd been talking about how much he wanted to do it when the little old man walked in and said hello to us just as if we were all old friends and were glad to see him. I wasn't glad, but Dorgan was.

"We've been discussing you," he said.

"So?" asked the little old man.

"Yes," said Dorgan, "I want to paint you. Will you sit for me?"

"Why, it would be a pleasure," said the little old man.

He tried all the poses Dorgan suggested and was so patient about it I almost forgot what he was. Dorgan was too excited to think of anything else but his chance. He finally got the little old man in the pose he wanted and started to work. He worked for an hour without saying anything.

The little old man sat perfectly still and his expression had never been milder. He looked almost kind and anyone not knowing him would of thought he was the godfather of all the Boy Scouts in the United States. I couldn't tell by Dorgan's expression how the thing was coming. He was concentrating everything he had on the job and painting like fury, afraid the little old man might not come back again.

Finally the little old man stretched and yawned and got down off the chair.

"I must go now," he said. "I'll come again another time."

Dorgan looked disappointed.

"When?" he asked.

"Whenever it suits your convenience," said the little old man.

"Tomorrow?" asked Dorgan.

The little old man nodded and went away.

Dorgan sat looking at what he had done and rubbing his jaw with his hand. There was paint on his hand and he smeared it all over his face.

"Well?" I asked.

Dorgan turned and gazed solemnly at me.

"It's coming," he said. "It's coming rather too damned well, if you ask me."

"What do you mean?" I asked.

Dorgan stared at the blob of paint he had on the canvas.

"Something is coming out of him that scares me," he said. "There isn't enough down to know what the hell it is but anyway it scares me."

"Oh, quit being mysterious," I said. "Anything that's down there you put it there and how in hell could it scare you?"

Dorgan looked disgusted.

"I haven't any more control over this picture than you have," he said.

"Well," I said, "I was watching the little old man and I've never seen him look so pleasant."

"I know it," said Dorgan, "but there's something more than that. There's something behind it all and it's coming out on the canvas."

The little old man sat only half an hour the second day and only fifteen minutes the third. What Dorgan had still didn't look like anything to me but he got more and more nervous and every time he looked at the painting his eyes bugged out and he stared at it until I got his mind off it. He'd smoke cigarettes and walk up and down before the picture and swear under his breath and yell for me to pour him another drink.

"Maybe," he said, "maybe the next time I'll have the little old man's secret. There's something there. Can't you see it?"

I looked again.

"No," I said, "I can't see anything."

"Look harder," he said.

I looked at the thing for a long time and finally it made me nervous.

"I don't know," I said. "Maybe there's something. Maybe it's the way you mix your paints."

"You're blind and you're a fool," Dorgan told me.

The next time the little old man came in for a sitting I watched him closely. At first he was just a mild little old duck sitting uncomfortably in a chair and being damned patient about it. And then I got the idea the way he looked wasn't the way he felt at all. I got the notion he was making fun of Dorgan. I don't know how I got this notion. The little old man's expression hadn't changed any. I just felt it.

Dorgan painted slowly at first and finally he was breathing hard and painting like a house afire. His hands shook and he was making jabs at the canvas with his paint-brush. You'd have thought he was trying to poke holes in it. He'd look up quickly and stab at the canvas and pick up another brush and stab again. Then he'd study the little old man for five minutes before he'd turn back to the picture.

He looked up at me and his face was white. "Pour me a drink," he said.

I got him a drink and his hands shook as he took it from me. He gulped it down and went back to work.

All of a sudden he pushed the easel away from him and threw his paint-brush to the floor.

"All right," he said to the little old man. "I'm through."

The little old man turned slowly and looked at him.

"Quite through?" he asked.

"Yes," said Dorgan. "I'm through, damnit! Now get the hell out."

The little old man got down from the chair and stretched.

"May I look at the picture?" he asked.

Dorgan didn't say anything. The little old man walked over and gazed at the picture and shook his head and stroked his chin.

"An excellent likeness," he said. "May I congratulate you?"

Dorgan's fists were doubled up and he was shaking.

"Get out," he said.

The little old man darted him a quick look and Dorgan stepped back.

"Oh, very well," he said. "Shall I come back?"

"No," said Dorgan. "For Lord's sake, no. Stay away."

"If it so pleases me," said the little old man.

He looked at the picture awhile longer, shrugged, and went out. Dorgan sat down and asked me to get him a drink. I got him the drink and then went to look at the picture. I'd seen some of it while Dorgan was working but I couldn't tell what it was like because he was always in the way.

So when I walked up to it and got a good look at it, it was like seeing something horrible in the dark. It was like something in a dream, something that scares you and when you wake up you're still scared but you can't remember exactly what the thing was that scared you.

It was the little old man all right, but there was something else besides just a picture of him. There was something jumped out at you and startled you. At first you might say: "Why, it's just a little old man," and then you'd gasp and you'd think: "My God! That's the most evil thing I've ever seen."

"Good Lord!" I said.

"That's him," said Dorgan. "That's the little old man in the flesh. It's him in the flesh and what's more, Johnny, it's his dark, malignant little soul."

28

Pete was washing the windows of our apartment and Dorgan and I were discussing the little old man. Pete was doing a deliberately sloppy job just to let me know he still blamed me for the scare the little old man had thrown into him. He was standing on the window-sills with his body outside. The windows were pulled partly up and partly down and he was hanging onto the top parts while he washed with one hand.

Dorgan asked him to have a drink but he just shook his head and didn't answer.

Dorgan and I were trying to decide what to do about the little old man. We'd thought we should do something for a long time but it wasn't until Dorgan painted the picture of him that we made up our minds we had to make up our minds what to do.

"Maybe we could catch him and tie him up and have a psychiatrist in to examine him," said Dorgan. "If he was declared insane we could have him shipped to Napa or Stockton."

"Sure," I said, "if we can have him declared insane."

"Well, he is," said Dorgan.

"Yes," I said, "but not in the way that'd mean anything to a psychiatrist. If we were to have him examined he'd play possum and the alienist'd think we were trying to railroad someone."

"That's right," said Dorgan.

"At that," I said, "maybe we could hire a psychiatrist to say he's crazy."

"You mean get a crooked one?" asked Dorgan.

"Just a run-of-the-mill psychiatrist," I said. "I mean the kind they use in murder trials. The kind that get together, choose up sides, and testify on opposite sides of the question of the defendant's sanity. We might get one of those."

"I don't think so," said Dorgan. "Those babies aren't unethical when they do that; they're just rooting for the home team. We'd have to get the little old man in court before we could buy a really worth-while psychiatrist's testimony."

We discussed other plans and none of them seemed any good. While we were at it, the little old man came in.

"I thought I'd have a look at my portrait," he said.

"It's in the other room under the davenport with its face to the floor," said Dorgan.

The little old man went in and got the portrait and came out and propped it up on the table. He drew up a chair and started looking at his picture. He didn't pay any attention to us. Dorgan and I tried to talk about something else but we couldn't. We both started staring first at the little old man and then at his picture. I felt uneasy and so did Dorgan.

I tried to imagine myself getting up and grabbing him and I knew I couldn't do it.

"I couldn't do it even with Dorgan's help," I thought. "I couldn't touch him."

The little old man looked up and saw Pete hanging onto the window with his body leaning out over the courtyard five stories below. He got up and walked toward the window and Pete saw him. Pete's eyes got big and his legs trembled.

"He might fall," the little old man said.

He was gazing innocently and absently at Pete and his voice was casual but there was something made me jerk straight in my chair and look at Dorgan.

"I don't see why he should," said Dorgan. "He's been doing it for years and he hasn't fallen yet."

I could tell Dorgan was nervous, too.

The little old man dragged a chair to where he could sit in it and watch Pete at work.

"There's always a first time," he said.

His expression was as bland as a kid watching a man paint a fence.

"Oh sure," said Dorgan. "There's always a first time."

The little old man glanced at his portrait.

"I take it you do not like my picture," he said.

"I like it well enough," said Dorgan.

The little old man grinned maliciously.

"It wasn't a very prominent hanging you gave it," he said.

"Not very," said Dorgan.

We were sitting on our chairs waiting for him to go.

Pete rubbed the window with nervous jerks of his hand and when he inched along the sill you could see his legs were trembling. He was gripping the upper edge of the window so tightly his knuckles were white. I knew he wanted to get out of the little old man's sight but to do it he would have had to climb back into the room and he was too afraid to do that.

"If some tough Italian had threatened Pete with a knife and he came in here, Pete would break the window to get at him," I thought. "The little old man hasn't threatened him or done anything to him and yet Pete's so scared he's about to fall off the window-ledge."

The little old man turned to me.

"I would appreciate a sherry," he said.

I wanted to tell him to go to hell but what I did was get up and go into the kitchen. Dorgan followed me and we looked at one another but we didn't say anything. We both had a stiff shot of whisky and I poured the little old man a sherry and took it to him. He was sitting in his chair looking closely at Pete.

Everything happened so fast I didn't get the picture a scene at a time but all in a blur and I couldn't tell what'd happened first and what second. Pete's face went white and his eyes bugged out and his knuckles got whiter and whiter on the window-edge and they began slipping. His legs were inside the room, dangling. Then his body went over backward and the last thing I saw of him was his feet going out the window.

Dorgan and I ran out and caught the elevator and went into the courtyard through the basement. Pete was all huddled up on the cement and when we tried to lift him his body sagged in the middle. Dorgan and I did the usual damn fool things people do when there's a man dying. We rubbed Pete's wrists and tried to talk him into opening his eyes so's he could tell us he really wasn't going to die.

I don't know how long the little old man had been there. I didn't notice him until Pete's body jerked and he opened his eyes. Pete didn't see anything at first. Then the little old man stooped over and looked down at him and Pete's eyes got wide and he shrieked like a hysterical woman.

Then his body got limp again and he was dead.

Pete's wife heard the shriek and she came out and his shriek hadn't died away before she was making the same kind of noise and it seemed he was still shrieking.

When we got calm enough to look around the little old man was gone.

29

Dorgan and I were alone in the apartment drinking and all we could drink didn't wipe out the blurred sight of Pete falling off the ledge. We drank whisky by the water-glass and still we could hear Pete's shriek when he opened his eyes just before he died. We talked as loudly as we could and we still could hear Pete's wife crying in her basement apartment.

"I don't know what to do," I kept saying.

"And neither do I," said Dorgan, "But we've got to do something."

We'd be silent awhile and then we'd start talking about it again.

"Pete must have got so scared he just let go," said Dorgan.

"I don't think that's the way it was," I said. "The scareder he got, the harder he hung onto the window. It was something else."

"Well, the little old man didn't push him," said Dorgan. "He was sitting over there before Pete fell."

"I know it," I said. "But just the same the little old man had something to do with it."

"Of course he did," said Dorgan. "But prove it. Prove it so's a cop would believe you."

"That's the trouble," I said. "We can't prove anything because we don't know anything for sure."

Dorgan gulped a drink and held the glass in front of him and stared across the room. I followed his gaze but I didn't see anything. Dorgan got up and stopped and picked up a bar of soap from where it'd been half hidden beneath a couch.

He looked at it a long time and his face got white. He handed it to me without saying anything. On the bar of soap there was a mark that made me understand everything that'd happened. Pete'd stepped on it and it'd thrown him off balance and then skidded from under his foot and shot into the room.

"The soap was on the other window-sill," said Dorgan. "I saw it. I remember distinctly."

"I know," I said. "I saw it too."

Dorgan sat down and clenched his fists and started banging them together.

"That settles it," he said.

"It sure does," I said. "He committed a murder and we saw it happen."

"Next time we see him," said Dorgan, "we won't say anything. We'll just knock him down and tie him up and call a cop."

"We'll have to," I said, "even if the cop won't believe us."

"We'll make the cop believe us," said Dorgan.

"What if he won't?" I asked.

"We'll figure that out later," said Dorgan.

"We haven't any proof it was the little old man put the soap there," I said. "And it'd be hard proving he intended to murder Pete even if he did."

Dorgan glared at me.

"Do you think the little old man put the soap there for the deliberate purpose of murdering Pete?" he asked.

"Sure," I said. "I know he did."

"Well," said Dorgan, "that's what we'll have to make somebody believe. This can't go on forever."

"I know it," I said. "It can't go on even for a little while longer. I'm not kidding myself. I don't believe he likes us any more than he did Pete."

Dorgan paced the floor.

"The way he looks at us proves that," he said.

"He's always figuring things out when he looks at us," I said.

"Yes," said Dorgan, "he's figuring out an extra-startling method of amusing himself with us."

"Well," I said, "we've got to do something."

"We sure have," said Dorgan.

30

The little old man didn't show up and so Dorgan and I went out looking for him. We went out looking for him and we hoped we wouldn't find him. We weren't any too damned sure what we would do if we did find him. We told one another what we'd do but we knew that didn't mean we'd do it when the time came. We didn't find the little old man and finally we decided we didn't really want to find him and the best thing for us to do was to go away from San Francisco.

Dorgan said he'd stay if I stayed and he'd go with me if I went and that I'd be a damned fool to stay. Dorgan wanted to go as much as I did. We didn't kid one another about being brave. We were both afraid and we admitted it.

I went to the park three nights in a row and Trelia didn't show up. When I finally caught her she was swimming and the water was warm and she didn't come out for a long while. I sat on the bank and smoked cigarettes and tried to tell myself the conversation'd take a different turn than I knew it would take.

Finally she crawled out and sat beside me and shook her hair and splashed me with water and laughed when I ducked.

"Why don't you come in and swim with me?" she asked.

"I haven't got a bathing-suit," I said.

"You don't need one," she said.

"Oh yes I do," I said.

"Why?" she asked.

"You're naked like a child," I thought, "and if I were naked I'd be naked like a man and I'd feel ashamed. If you were naked like a woman I wouldn't feel ashamed. So I won't go swimming with you."

"Oh, I don't want to swim," I said out loud.

"It's fun," she said.

"I'm going away, Trelia," I said.

She fooled with her hair and didn't seem to have heard me.

"I'm going away," I said.

"Yes?" she said.

"Yes," I said. "I may be gone for a long time."

She didn't say anything.

"Don't you care?" I asked.

"I've been trying to think," she said. "I guess I'll miss you. You're nice to talk to."

"Will you miss me very much?" I asked.

"I don't think so," she said.

"I'll miss you," I said.

"Then why are you going?" she asked.

"Because I'm afraid," I said.

I told her about the little old man.

"So you see I have to go," I said.

"Yes," she said. "I see."

"Why don't you come with me?" I asked.

"Go with you?" she asked. "Where?"

"Oh, any place," I said.

She shook her head.

"I won't leave my lake," she said. "Why do you want me to come?"

"Because I'm afraid for you," I said. "The little old man knows you're here. He might—You'll have to come, Trelia."

She shook her head again.

"No," she said. "I'm not afraid of him. He's nice to me. He likes my flowers. He wouldn't hurt me."

It was no use trying to convince her the little old man might harm her. She wouldn't believe me.

"That isn't all," I said. "I want you to come with me for other reasons, Trelia."

"What other reasons?" she asked.

"Simply because I want you to be with me," I said. "Don't you want to be with me?"

She considered this awhile and finally shook her head.

"No," she said. "I didn't like you so much in your apartment. I just like you here."

"Don't you care if you never see me again?" I asked.

"A little," she said.

"But not enough to come with me?" I said.

"No," she said.

"Well," I said, "maybe that's the best idea."

"Why?" she asked.

"Because," I said, "seeing you and wanting you to be with me and having you say you don't care very much whether or not you ever see me again isn't much fun."

"I'm sorry," she said.

"So I guess we'll just say good-by and that'll be the end of it," I said.

I got up and she got up and she stood beside me naked and glistening with drops of water still beaded on her white skin and I wondered if I ever could say good-by and mean it and what would happen to me if I did. I asked her to kiss me and she held her face up to me and I pushed her away.

"No, don't," I said.

She turned and dived into the lake and swam under water awhile and then came up and continued on across the lake.

31

"It's damned goofy, this," said Dorgan. "We're two grown men and we're not superstitious and I suppose we've got guts enough to stand up and fight in case it's necessary and here we're running away from a little old man one of us could beat hell out of with one hand."

"It sure is," I said. "It sure is goofy."

Dorgan and I were packing our things and doing it in a hurry. Now we'd decided to go we wanted to get it over with in a hurry.

"But I don't see what else we can do," said Dorgan.

"Neither do I," I said.

I kept on packing and thinking of the little old man and Trelia, and the more I thought of Trelia, the slower I packed. I finally stopped and held a sock in my hand and looked at it as if it were an interesting book. Dorgan shoved some shirts into his suitcase.

"Yessir," he said. "It sure is goofy."

"It sure is," I said. "The goofiest thing about it is I'm not going."

Dorgan looked surprised.

"The hell you aren't," he said. "Why?"

"Well," I said, "I'm getting sick of all this. I'm going to stay here and face things out. No little old man's going to chase me out of town."

Dorgan's eyes squinted and the freckles started skidding up and down his nose.

"This sudden change of mind," he said, "it hasn't anything to do with Trelia by any chance, has it?"

"Not a thing," I said. "I'm just not going to run away, that's all."

"That's what I thought," said Dorgan. "You've made up your mind it's no use your seeing Trelia any more because it only upsets you and you wouldn't change your mind on a sensible decision like that."

"That's about the way it is," I said.

"You're a liar," said Dorgan.

"I know it," I said.

32

It didn't make any difference, my deciding not to go away. Ten minutes after I'd decided two hard-bitten men walked in. They kept their hands in their pocket while they looked us over.

"Which one of you guys is John Price?" one of them asked.

"I am," I said, "and which one of you birds think you have the right to walk into a fellow's apartment without knocking?"

"Me," said the first fellow. "I'm both of 'em. So you're John Price?"

"Yes," I said. "What of it?"

He walked over and took a look at the suitcases I'd been packing.

"Just in time," he said to the other fellow. "He was getting ready to lam out."

"Will you tell me what the hell this is all about and why the hell you shouldn't beat it?" I asked.

The second fellow grinned.

"You wouldn't know, would you?" he asked.

"No, I wouldn't," I said.

"He can't understand," the fellow said to his companion. "He's dumb, this baby is. Do you think he can read?"

"Read what?" I asked.

"This warrant," the first fellow said. "It's a warrant for your arrest. And, in case you haven't guessed it, we're policemen. Wanna see our stars?"

"My arrest for what?" I asked.

"Think hard," the second policeman said. "Think back as far as last night. Did you park your car by a fireplug, or spit on the sidewalk, or cross the street against the red light?"

"Or just casually happen to bump a guy off?" the other policeman said.

"What the hell you talking about?" I asked. "Who bumped who off?"

"Well," said the first policeman, "in case you're in the habit of killing strangers, we'll tell you the guy's name. His name's George Grady."

"You mean the bartender?" I asked.

"Oh, so you do know him?" the second policeman said. "Yes, that's the guy was murdered."

"My God!" I said.

"What happened to George?" Dorgan asked.

The first policeman turned to him.

"Oh, you know George, too," he said. "Say, Tim, anything on the warrant about picking up two guys?"

"Just one," said the other policeman.

"We'll be back for you later," said the first policeman.

He grabbed me by the arm and pulled a gun.

"Come nice and quiet?" he asked.

"Or shall we beat your can in?" the other policeman asked.

I was sick all over. I hadn't done anything but the fact I was being arrested made me feel half guilty. I was as afraid as if I really had killed someone.

"You can't take me," I said.

Without a word the first policeman smashed me in the mouth and knocked me half-way across the room. Dorgan jumped at him, and the second policeman let him have it behind the ear with the butt of his revolver. Dorgan went down in a heap.

"That," said the second policeman, "is what you call resisting arrest. We'd better take 'em both in."

They handcuffed me and then handcuffed Dorgan while he was still unconscious. The first policeman got a pitcher of water and sloshed it on Dorgan and he came to. He swore at the policemen and one of them kicked him in the ribs.

"No use putting up a fight," I said. "We'll have to go along. The fools've probably got the wrong address but anyway they've got us and if we argue they'll beat our heads off."

"You said it," said the first policeman.

They put us in a police car and one policeman rode with me in back and one rode with Dorgan in front. Blood was trickling down Dorgan's collar and he was still groggy. My lips were puffing up and bleeding inside.

"You fellows're making a damned fool mistake," I said.

The policeman with me laughed.

"Maybe," he said, "but the last time I read my police book, it said it was against the law to shoot bartenders in the back."

"I didn't shoot him," I said.

"Warrant says you did," he said.

"Hell with your warrant," I said. "I didn't do it. I'll prove it when I get to the station and then we'll see about you fellows beating up innocent persons."

The policeman caught me by the collar and shook me.

"Listen, smart guy," he said, "if you are innocent I wouldn't get any more done to me for hitting you twice than I would for hitting you just once. Shut your trap or I'll give you these."

His red knuckles were wagging within an inch of my nose.

"And besides I think you're guilty and for two cents I'd sock you whether you said anything or not," he said.

I kept still. I kept still and wondered how the little old man fitted into what was happening. The policemen hadn't mentioned him but I knew he was in the thing somewhere.

33

They hauled us into the police station and separated us. Three policemen went into one room with Dorgan and I was taken into another with a captain, a sergeant, and a plain-clothes officer. They had me sit down and they sat around me and smoked with their hats tipped back on their heads. They started out talking in a calm tone of voice.

"Now come clean, Price," the captain said. "It won't do you any good holding out on us. That way you'll only make us sore, and the sorer you make us, the harder we'll go on you. Why did you do it?"

"Why did I do what?" I asked.

"Why did you kill Grady?" he asked. "Have a beef with him about money? A horse-race bet? What was it?"

"I didn't kill him," I said.

"Oh, can the innocence stuff," said the sergeant. "We got the goods on you. Quit stalling."

The captain turned to him.

"Let me handle this," he said. "The man's upset. He has to have time to make up his mind. He looks intelligent. I know he'll come clean soon."

He placed his hand on my knee.

"Come on, son," he said, "get it off your chest. You'll feel better. I know you will. What was it, self-defense, maybe?"

"No," I said.

"I'll say it wasn't," said the sergeant. "How'n hell can you shoot a man in the back and call it self-defense?"

The captain was trying to trap me and he was sore at the sergeant for butting in.

"Keep your bazoo shut until I ask you to open it," he said. "If you insist on hanging your trap on a hinge go out in the hall and catch flies; there's lots out there."

He smiled at me.

"Don't mind him," he said. "I'm your friend. I always feel sorry for young fellows that get themselves in pickles like this. Too much booze, son?"

"Listen, Captain," I said, "you're wasting your time. I didn't kill George Grady. I didn't know he was killed until your men came up and socked me and showed me a warrant. What gave you the notion I'm guilty?"

"Well," said the captain, "we have a lot of ways finding out things. You see, everything happens someone sees it."

"You mean you've got a witness?" I asked.

He grinned.

"You're guessing close," he said. "Maybe you thought nobody saw you sneak up Annie Alley behind Grady and plug him but somebody did."

"Sneak up Annie Alley?" I said. "Why, I wasn't even anywheres around there last night."

"Maybe we are mistaken," the captain said. "Just where were you?"

"Well," I said, "my friend was busy painting and I wandered out to find a place to eat and I ran onto a Mexican place called One-Eyed Chili's and I had dinner there and went straight home."

The captain looked up at the sergeant.

"Sure," said the sergeant. "I know the place. It's about three blocks from Annie Alley. Annie Alley's only three blocks long. So this guy was right near where it happened."

The captain turned to me.

"There you see, son," he said, "it's no use lying. You trapped yourself."

He turned to the sergeant.

"Sell liquor in One-Eyed Chili's?" he asked.

"Sure," said the sergeant, "Mexican, imported, bootleg. Everything. Great place for souses."

The captain put his hand on my knee again.

"Come clean now, son," he said. "Get drunk in there, did you?"

"No," I said. "I didn't have a drink."

"Now I'll tell you how it happened," he said. "You had it in for Grady and you knew he passed Annie Alley on his way to catch a street car. So you went into the Mex's and got soused getting up enough nerve to pop him off. You got soused and you popped him off. Isn't that so?"

"No," I said, "it isn't so. It's damned silly. It might be a coincidence I was eating near where he was killed but that doesn't mean I killed him."

"It wasn't a coincidence he happened to be in front of your bullet," said the sergeant.

"The sergeant's right," said the captain. "Your alibi's shot to hell, kid. Come clean now. Fess up. You'll feel better."

"You're wasting your time, I tell you, Captain," I said. "You can talk to doomsday but you won't hang something on me I didn't do."

"How about the witness?" asked the captain.

"Witness my ear," I said. "That's either a bluff or a frame-up. You can't scare me."

The captain quit smiling. He got up and shifted his cigar and squinted through the smoke at me and all of a sudden slapped my face with a hand big's a first baseman's glove.

"Frame-up, eh?" he said.

He batted me again and I kicked at him and the sergeant let me have one with his fist and when I tried to get up the plain-clothes officer walked over and kicked me in the stomach. They held me and slapped me and shouted at me and threatened me but they couldn't make me admit I'd killed George.

Sometimes I felt like doing it, though. They gave me an awful going over.

They gave Dorgan one, too. When they took me out to book me, Dorgan came staggering out. He had a black eye and his nose was bleeding. One of the cops who came out with him had a smashed lip.

They asked some questions and booked me and started to lead me off.

"What they doing to you?" I asked Dorgan.

"Decided I didn't have anything to do with it," he said. "But they tried to execute me first."

"Resisted arrest," said one of the policemen.

"I'll get you an attorney," said Dorgan. "They can't keep you in here."

"Get him two," said the police captain. "He'll need 'em."

Dorgan tried to talk with me some more but they pushed him away and took me to my cell. They locked me in alone and went away and I shouted for awhile until I realized it was silly. I sat down and tried to tell myself this wasn't happening and it couldn't happen. But I knew it had happened and I was afraid of what else might happen. I was scared. Being arrested made me feel guilty of something and being in a cell all by myself made me feel even more guilty.

"They'll cross-question me and I'll get balled up and convict myself," I thought.

I got a little calmer.

"Don't be a fool," I told myself. "They can't get you rattled, because you didn't do anything. My God! They can't pin a murder on you. You never did own a gun."

And then I started thinking about the little old man and I didn't feel so sure.

34

The next morning the captain and the sergeant came and got me and took me into an office. They asked me again would I come clean and when I said no they called in three fellows dressed in ordinary clothes. They had me stand against the wall with them.

"What's the idea?" I asked.

"Got a witness to identify you as the murderer," said the captain.

"Swell idea," I said; "these three eggs've got their hats on and they're smoking. It'd be easy for your witness to pick out a fellow without a hat and not smoking."

The captain had the others take off their hats and put out their cigarettes. Then he pressed a button and a policeman came in.

"Get the witness," said the captain.

There was a long wait and finally I heard footsteps coming down the hall. I knew who it was before he came in. It was the little old man. He came in holding his hat in his hand and blinking his eyes and looking nervous.

"Now, sir," said the captain, "I want you to take a careful look at those men against the wall over there and tell me if you've ever seen any of them before."

The little old man took a step forward and blinked his eyes and then pointed to me. I jumped as if he'd pointed a pistol at me.

"I've seen that man before," he said.

"The rest of you fellows can beat it," said the captain. "Thanks."

The others got their hats and went away. The captain and the sergeant and the little old man stayed.

"Now tell me where you saw this man before?" said the captain.

"Oh, I've seen him a number of places, sir," said the little old man. "Mostly in the bar where Mr. Grady worked, though."

He was talking in an apologetic tone of voice.

"I know," said the captain, "but where did you see him last?"

"At the west entrance to Annie Alley, sir," said the little old man.

"Are you sure?" asked the captain.

"Oh yes, sir," said the little old man. "He stood under a street light and I saw him quite plainly. It was he I saw. I could not have been mistaken."

"All right," said the captain, "tell us what happened."

The little old man glanced blandly at me, then turned to the captain.

"Well," he said, "I dislike very much having to endanger the life of a fellowman, even a murderer."

"Cut that," said the captain. "It's your duty."

"Well, sir," said the little old man, "I thought this man acted suspiciously, so I stood across the street and watched him, not having anything else to do. After a while Mr. Grady came along and Price there turned his back so that Mr. Grady couldn't see his face. When Mr. Grady turned into the alley Price followed him. He pulled a gun and shot and then threw it down and ran away."

The little old man looked at me and there was a malicious glitter in his eye.

He was apologetic again when he turned to the captain.

"I was so shocked I didn't know what to do," he said. "It was some time before I came to my senses enough to call a policeman. By that time Price had escaped. I hope you will forgive me for waiting until this morning until I made up my mind it was my duty to inform on Price."

"Should have told everything you knew last night," said the captain. "He might have got away. But it's all right."

The little old man pulled a handkerchief out of his pocket and wiped his forehead with it and looked into my eyes. His lips were slightly curled and you could almost see the tip of his tongue licking his lips in satisfaction. He held the handkerchief in front of him and his hand shook.

"I'd almost forgotten this," he said.

"What?" asked the captain.

"This handkerchief," said the little old man.

"He threw it away when he was running."

I'd been so dazed I hadn't said a word but now that I knew how far the little old man'd gone with the thing, I jumped across the room at him. The sergeant hit me across the face with a blackjack and I staggered back against the wall.

The captain took the handkerchief and looked at it.

"Initials're J. P.," he said. "John Price, eh? Nice bit of evidence this. Used it to cover up fingerprints."

He turned to the little old man.

"You can go," he said, "but see you stay where we can get you, else we'll have to lock you up as a material witness."

"Oh, I'll not go away, sir," said the little old man.

He hesitated at the door.

"You know I would feel sorry for this man if it weren't for—"

He hesitated and darted me a look of evil self-satisfaction.

"If it wasn't for what?" asked the captain.

"Well, if it wasn't for him getting drunk and bragging how he killed Albert E. Bagley," he said.

"*What?*" the captain said.

He jumped out of his chair and grabbed the little old man by the arm. The little old man seemed startled by the captain's excitement.

"Oh, I don't think he did it, sir," he said. "But he seemed to take a delight in discussing the crime and when I saw what I did last night I thought it over and decided he was a dangerous man, maybe a lunatic and—"

"Never mind what you thought," said the captain. "What about him bragging about killing Bagley?"

"Well," said the little old man, "he'd get drunk and buy George, the bartender, drinks and then he'd tell George how he killed Bagley."

The captain's eyes were popping with excitement.

"Oh, he told Grady about it, eh?" he said.

"Yes, sir," said the little old man, "and he'd tell Grady if he peeped—that's the word he used, I think—he'd kill him."

It seemed the captain was going to do a handspring for joy. He laughed and pounded his thighs with his big hands and walked back and forth across the room.

"Two birds," he said, "two little birdies with one stone. Oh Lord! Two birds."

"You've got to listen to me, captain," I said. "That man there killed Bagley himself."

The captain stopped and grinned at me.

"Oh, the little old geezer here did the killings?" he said. "He kill Grady, too?"

"I'm sure of it," I said. "Go on, give him the works like you did me. Pound it out of him."

I was scared out of my wits. I knew I was making things worse for myself. I could feel the sweat rolling down into the cuts from the beatings I'd taken.

"You've got to, do you hear me!" I yelled. "He did it himself. He's crazy, I tell you. Don't let him get away."

The little old man stood against the wall and stared steadily at me. His eyes grew wider and they turned green and started flickering.

35

And then they turned loose on me. The newspapers and the police and the radio and the public. They held the little old man as a material witness for a few days and then they turned him loose because they were convinced he was an honest, harmless old fellow who wouldn't think of not being where he could be found when they wanted him to testify. The reporters interviewed him and told what a fine-looking old man he was and how he at first hated to turn me in and how he was now convinced he had done only his duty.

The little old man was a hero. Dorgan tried to explain what he really was like and the police threatened to lock him up and the newspapers had a three-day holiday over the story he gave them. They had long stories about how Johnny Price's friend'd tried to save him from the gallows with the weirdest, most cockeyed story since *Gulliver's Travels* and the *Arabian Nights*.

The police and the newspapers built up what looked like a perfect case against me.

I was a parlor Communist, they said, and I hated Albert Bagley, the publisher, because he was conducting a campaign against radicals. I killed Bagley and then I got so I was haunted by what I'd done and I took to drinking and I had to tell someone about the crime, so I spilled it all to George, the bartender. When I'd get sober I'd worry about George squealing on me and I'd threaten him. Finally he said he was going to spill his stuff to the police and I trailed him and killed him.

"For God's sake," Captain Harrelson told me, "I hate to see a guy hanged without putting up a fight, even a half-baked rat like you. Start figuring out a defense or an alibi, you fool, else they'll have you hung before the jury gets its first free meal. Blaming the thing on the little old geezer ain't going to help you none."

That's the way my attorney felt about it. He thought I was lying and he was sore because I wouldn't invent a better alibi. He wanted me to plead insanity and when I wouldn't he threatened to give up the case.

"All right," he said at last, "it's your funeral, not mine. I'll do my best but I'm warning you we can't get to first base if you stick to your cockeyed story."

So that's the kind of a lawyer I had and that's the kind of defense I was going to get.

I was as good as hanged. It was the word of the little old man and a handkerchief he'd stolen from me. And the lads at San Quentin were dusting out a death cell and the fellow who got twenty-five dollars and three days off for serving as hangman was already planning on what he was going to do with his vacation.

The prosecution wasn't going to aim at the Bagley murder. They didn't have any witnesses for that. The little old man hadn't said he'd seen me do it. But they were going to use it as a motive for my killing Grady. The newspapers had been banging at the police because they hadn't solved the Bagley murder and if they convicted me for the Grady murder, then they'd have both cases cleared up.

I'd pace back and forth in my cell and start remembering the thing from the first—from the day Bagley was killed—and I'd say to myself: "Love of God! They can't do it. They *can't* do it. This is a sane world and the people in it are sane and something will happen to stop this whole insane business. Something will happen to stop them from hanging you."

But nothing happened. Things kept shaping out more and more so's to give the district attorney an easy job. It couldn't happen. But that's the way it was. They were fixing to hang me.

36

At first they held me incommunicado but after the arraignment and preliminary hearing, they let me have visitors. A couple of reporters came and I wouldn't talk to them. Then some fellows came around claiming to know me but all they wanted was a look at a man who had his name and picture in the newspapers every day.

Finally Dorgan talked his way in and he sat across the visitors' table from me and a policeman watched us and heard everything we said.

Dorgan looked five years older. He didn't grin any more and his lips were pressed close together and he talked with his teeth held together.

"I'm trying," he told me. "I'm trying hard to do something, Johnny. But the more I try, the worse I make things. The newspapers laugh at me and I can't get a good attorney to listen to me. I've hired detectives but they can't do anything. What's the use shadowing the little old man? He's behaving like a Sunday-school superintendent and when anyone talks to him he beams as if he had a heart big's a basketball and used it double shifts to love the world."

"I know, Dorgan," I said. "What we were afraid of has happened. The little old man's got us. Anyway, he's got me."

"Which makes me feel fine," said Dorgan. "Here you're my friend and you're in a trap and all I can do is shove you in deeper. If I can find that little devil alone I'm going to choke him to death even if it doesn't do any good."

"You wouldn't be able to do it," I said.

Dorgan nodded gloomily.

"I know it," he said.

"And besides it wouldn't do any good," I said.

"I suppose not," Dorgan said.

They wouldn't let Dorgan in very often and in the meanwhile I sat on my cot and held my head and wondered when the thing that was whirling inside'd get going fast enough to split it open. I went over what'd happened again and again and I started thinking of what it'd be like to be hanged and I realized that maybe pretty soon my attorney could plead me insane and even the prosecution'd have a hard time hiring a psychiatrist who'd say it wasn't so.

I thought of Trelia mostly, though. Now I was alone and it seemed I'd either go crazy or be hanged she seemed more and more important to me and I wondered how I could ever have even thought of leaving her, even if she wasn't interested in me and there were things about her made me uncomfortable when I was with her. I realized there were other things about her wouldn't ever let me be happy when I was away from her.

I'd shut my eyes and see her standing in the moonlight with the water beaded on her white skin and her girl's face turned up to mine and her eyes looking interested and amazed and merry and doubtful. Then I'd see her body curving off into the lake and splitting the black water and her coming up and swimming and calling back at me over her shoulder.

I got so I couldn't stand that thought any more than the others. I'd never see her again, I told myself, and thinking of her only made it that much worse.

I kept nagging Dorgan to find out about her and he'd go out to the lake at night and wouldn't have any luck. I finally decided maybe I really was crazy, that I'd been crazy all the time and had just imagined Trelia and that maybe I'd been so crazy that maybe the police were right and I really had killed Bagley and Grady.

37

When the little old man suddenly appeared at the bars of my cell, I wasn't a bit surprised. I'd been expecting him. I didn't wonder how he'd managed to get past the guards. I'd stopped wondering how he accomplished anything.

"How do you do?" he said.

He stood near the bars and peered mildly at me and you'd have thought he was some old fellow'd found me on a park bench and wanted to start a conversation about the weather.

"You going through with this?" I asked.

He looked surprised.

"With what?" he asked.

"This frame-up," I said. "You going to let them hang me?"

"Hang you?" he said.

"Yes, hang me," I said.

"Are they going to hang you, then?" he asked.

He wasn't smiling but the amusement he was getting out of the interview showed in his eyes.

"You know damned well they are," I said. "You going to let them?"

He shrugged and spread out his hands.

"Why, my dear young friend," he said, "you attribute to me more extraordinary powers than I possess. How could I stop them?"

I walked close to the bars.

"By telling the truth," I said.

"The truth?" he asked.

"Yes," I said. "By admitting you lied. By telling them I didn't kill Bagley."

"That's right," he said. "You didn't kill Bagley, did you? You didn't kill him because it was I who did."

"Yes," I said, "and you killed Grady, too."

He nodded.

"So I did," he said.

"And they're hanging it on me," I said.

"So they are," he said.

"Are you going to let them hang me?" I asked.

"Well," he said, "I'm not going to stop them." I reached my hands through the bars and tried to grab him but he stepped back. His eyes started growing larger and they turned green and flickered in anger.

I realized it wasn't going to do me any good to lose my temper.

"Why are you doing all this?" I asked.

"Perhaps it amuses me," he said.

"You've got to help me," I said.

"Why?" he asked.

"Because you can't let them hang an innocent man," I said. "You can't, that's all."

"Oh yes I can," he said.

I swore at him and tried again to reach him through the bars, and the more I swore, the more he seemed to be enjoying himself. At last I gave up.

"For God's sake go away, then," I said.

"Presently," he said.

I sat down on my cot and held my head in my hands. I didn't look at the little old man.

"I brought you something," he said.

"What?" I asked.

He stepped closer to the bars.

"This," he said.

He showed me a small package.

"What is it?" I asked.

"Poison," he said.

"Poison?" I asked.

"Yes," he said. "Do you want it?"

I started yelling again.

"No, I don't want it," I said. "Why should I?" He still held the package toward me.

"Why shouldn't you?" he asked.

"Go away," I said. "I don't want it."

"Then you'd rather be hanged?" he said. "You'd rather go through the suspense of a trial and then be placed in a cell in a department housing other condemned men and watch them go out one by one to be hanged and then follow them through the trap?"

I thought of calling for the guards but I was sure the little old man would be gone when they came.

He reached through the bars and placed the package on the floor and stared at me and then went away. I walked over and got the package and started to throw it away. And then I thought of what he'd said about the trial and the suspense and going through the trap and I hesitated. Finally I put the package in my pocket.

I walked up and down the cell and tried to decide what to do.

"Maybe he thinks they won't convict me, so he's going to make sure I'm destroyed," I thought.

And then I thought of how certain my own attorney was that I was going to be convicted and I took the package out and opened it and looked at the little bottle. I couldn't bring myself to pull the cork out. I just looked at the bottle and cursed the little old man.

38

I took the bottle out a number of times the next few days but I never pulled the cork. I knew if I did it would be like starting to fall on slippery ice. I wouldn't be able to stop myself. I would take the poison. I wanted to take it but I was afraid to do it. I was just as afraid not to do it. The little old man couldn't have figured out a better way of torturing me.

I was thinking a lot about the bottle when Dorgan came to see me. He was all excited and I had a wild hope for a minute that maybe he was going to tell me I was to be released. But it wasn't that.

"Good Lord," he said, "you should see her."

"Who?" I asked.

"Trelia," he said. "You wouldn't believe it."

"What about Trelia?" I asked.

"She came up last night," said Dorgan. "I thought there was something different about her when first I saw her. But it took me some time to find out what it was. Then I realized."

"For Lord's sake, Dorgan, quit being so damned mysterious," I said. "What's eating you?"

"When I realized," said Dorgan, "I made her sit down and I started painting her. She didn't want to pose. She was excited and nervous and that made it all the better. You know I couldn't paint her before because there was something missing? Well, she's got that something now. I painted for hours. God! What a subject!"

"What'd she go to the apartment for?" I asked.

Dorgan was thinking about his picture and I had to repeat the question to snap him out of it.

"Oh," he said, "to find out about you."

I gripped the railing and held on tight.

"Was she worried about me?" I asked.

He looked at me in astonishment.

"Why, of course," he said. "Worried's no name for it. The girl's almost frantic."

"Frantic?" I asked. "Frantic about me? You sure? You sure, Dorgan?"

"Sure," he said. "Why shouldn't she be?"

"You know," I said, "you know damned well, Dorgan, she wasn't a bit interested in me. She wasn't even sorry when she thought I was going away."

He laughed.

"Oh, of course you wouldn't realize," he said. "That's the change in her. That's why I was able to paint the best thing I've ever done last night."

"I wouldn't realize what?" I asked.

"Why," he said, "that she loves you."

It seemed the jail room was rocking back and forth and that I was being shoved from my stool.

"Loves me?" I said.

"Sure," he said. "That's what made her complete. She's a woman now, a woman in love and she's afraid and real grief has come to her and she's the most beautiful thing God ever made."

I wanted to believe him and I didn't want to argue or ask any questions that'd show Dorgan was making a mistake. But I had to know one thing.

"Then why doesn't she visit me?" I asked.

"She's got a complex about places like this," Dorgan explained. "She said seeing you like this would be like seeing the animals in the cages at the park and she couldn't stand it."

"And so that's how it is," I told myself. "Trelia loves you and, of course, you've loved her always and it would be about the grandest thing ever happened to you excepting for the fact they're going to take you out of here one of these days and hang you and you'll never see Trelia again."

Dorgan guessed what was going on in my head and he quit grinning and got serious and tried to make me believe something'd happen and I'd soon be out and everything would be all right. I knew he was just whistling in the dark. Me, I had quit whistling in the dark. I *knew*.

"Tell me about Trelia," I said. "Tell me about her and quit trying to kid me. We both know you're lying."

"It's like I said," said Dorgan. "She's the most beautiful thing God ever made. She's a woman and there's something in her eyes lets you know her soul has blossomed and filled her with a sweetness and tenderness such as only saints are supposed to have."

"And she loves me," I said.

"And she loves you," he said. "She's just found it out herself and the pain of it has given her a soul, and her soul has given her beauty unsurpassed."

I didn't say anything. I was thinking about how it would have been better had she not started to love me and if I had not found out about it, seeing that she did. That made being in jail all the worse; it made being hanged all the more unthinkable. Here I was being offered things I'd never hoped to have and I couldn't have them because the little old man had decided to amuse himself with me.

"She's a woman now all right," said Dorgan. "She's a woman in love and all the instincts that were dormant in her have been awakened. She's a woman fighting for the thing she loves."

"Fighting?" I said.

"Well," he said, "not physically perhaps. But mentally. She's determined she's going to help you somehow."

"Not much she can do," I said.

"No," said Dorgan, "there isn't."

39

The day before the trial, my attorney came in to see me, and his expression wasn't so gloomy as it had been. He was puzzled.

"Prosecution's asked for a delay," he told me. "Don't know what's up."

"Probably scaring up a couple more witnesses to swear I'm the guy committed the last pogrom in Palestine," I said.

"Something's up," he told me. "I'll try and find out. District attorney's worried."

"Me 'n' him both," I said. "I'm worried, too. I'm so damned worried my brain's whirling around like a pinwheel. Why in hell don't you do something?"

"What can I do?" he asked.

"How should I know?" I asked. "You're a good attorney. Or a bad one. I don't know which. Anyway you thought of things to do to get Hymie Daniels out of that murder rap. And he was guilty. Guilty as hell. I'm innocent. So why can't you do something for me?"

"Maybe you are innocent," he said. "I wouldn't know about that. But innocent or guilty you haven't got any defense. If you'll take my advice and plead insanity, there might be a chance."

"No sale," I said. "In the first place, if I plead insanity I don't think I could put it over. I may be goofy but I'm not insane yet. And even if they do swallow the plea, then what? They'll lock me in an asylum and the little old man—"

"What about the little old man?" he asked.

"I'm afraid of him," I said.

"Well," he said, "he can't get into the asylum after you, can he?"

"Maybe not," I said, "but there're people outside he can get at."

"Well," he said, "I wouldn't know what to do about that. I'll try to find out what's worrying the district attorney. Maybe we'll get a break. I don't know, though."

"Don't forget to send me a bill," I said.

"I'm doing all I can for you," he said.

"Sure," I said. "Will you hold my hand when they put me on the gallows?"

He went away and I was alone with more worry and fear than I'd ever thought any man could hold. I knew the little old man planned to do something to Trelia and I knew I couldn't do anything to help her. The police wouldn't believe anything I said about it. All I could do was prowl up and down my cell and curse the little old man.

They postponed the trial for a week and then for another week. Finally it leaked out what was the matter. My attorney came in and he was almost cheerful.

"Their witness," he said. "The little old man. He's missing. Can't find hide nor hair of him."

"And that means what?" I asked.

"Well," he said, "he was the principal witness. Without him they'll have a weak case. We'll have a better chance of beating them."

"That is if the little old man doesn't turn up," I said.

"Yes," he said, "if the little old man doesn't turn up."

"Don't worry," I said. "He'll turn up. He wants to see me hanged."

"Where do you suppose he is, then?" the attorney asked.

"Figuring out a way to kill somebody else," I said.

And then I thought of Trelia and I knew that's what the little old man'd been up to. He was doing something to her. I grabbed the bars and yelled at the attorney.

"You've got to get me out of here," I said. "Right now. What in hell are you good for anyway?"

He backed away and tried to calm me down and I kept cursing him and finally he went away and a guard came along and told me to shut my duck farm or he'd come in and give me a treatment with his sap.

40

They kept postponing the trial from week to week and finally the newspapers got interested and wanted to know what it was all about. The police and the district attorney stalled. They said they knew where the little old man was and they'd produce him almost any day now.

But they didn't. The little old man had disappeared. No one had seen him. No one had heard of him. Rewards were offered for information about him but all that came of that was that reward-hunters made life miserable for a flock of Civil War veterans and white-haired bums. Finally the offer was withdrawn.

The police tried to make out a case against me anyway but they couldn't get started. Without the little old man they were sunk and they knew it.

They tried again to make me confess and it didn't work. They gave Dorgan a going over in the hopes he'd admit he'd made away with the little old man and that failed, too.

Soon the newspapers started turning against the police. They began saying the police were trying to frame me on the testimony of an aged lunatic and it wasn't long before the public was with me.

The police were very disappointed when finally they had to let me go. If they could have cooked up any sort of charge against me, they'd have done it—even riding a bicycle on the sidewalks. But they couldn't and one day I walked out of the jail and Dorgan pounced on me and shook my hand and pounded my back. He had a taxicab waiting at the curb.

"Whew, but you're lucky," he said. "Horseshoes all over you."

"Sure I'm lucky," I said. "I'm an innocent man and they pick me up and beat me and keep me in a cell for a couple of months and then they let me go. I don't like that kind of luck."

"That's tough," said Dorgan, "but what if the little old man hadn't disappeared?"

"I wonder what happened to him," I said.

"I've got a hunch Trelia can tell you," said Dorgan.

41

And this is the way it happened. I found it out from Dorgan and from Trelia and I guess what they didn't supply.

There I was in jail and they were fixing to hang me and Trelia'd decided she loved me. She wanted to help me but she was only a woman and there didn't seem anything she could do about it. She quit swimming in her lake. She walked through the woods and she brooded and wouldn't talk to the squirrels or the birds. She wouldn't eat and she couldn't sleep and it seemed she was dying like a flower that's been uprooted from its soil.

She knew the little old man was the cause of what'd happened to me and it'd be him responsible if they hanged me. At first she thought of going to him and pleading with him but she realized it wouldn't do any good. Finally she got to thinking of him not as a man of flesh and blood but as a personification of evil and when she got around to that point she made up her mind to something.

She started swimming in her lake again and for a while the little old man didn't show up. Then one night she knew he was watching her. She didn't see him but she could feel him. She had a feeling as if the lake'd suddenly become full of crawling, slimy things, she said.

The next night the little old man came out of the shadows and sat on the bank and watched her. She swam closer and finally he spoke.

"Good evening," he said.

"Good evening," she said.

She caught a low branch and floated on her back near where he was sitting.

"Why do you want them to hang Johnny?" she asked.

He shrugged his shoulders.

"You wouldn't understand," he said.

"Why don't you make them stop?" she asked.

"Why should I?" he asked.

He stared blandly at her and for the first time in her life she felt rage. It wasn't the kind of anger she felt the time they were laughing at her seals. It was a rage that made her want to destroy the little old man.

"You're a vicious, cruel, evil thing," she said.

His eyes started growing larger and they began to flicker with green fire.

"Be careful," he said.

"And I hate you," she said.

He shook his head slowly.

"That's unfortunate," he said. "Very unfortunate. Those I hate fare badly. But those who hate me fare even worse."

He stared steadily at her.

"It will be a shame to destroy such beauty," he said.

His flickering green eyes sent a chill through Trelia and she felt her strength being sucked from her.

"Come up here," he said.

She tried not to, but something in the little old man's eyes made her obey. She climbed up on the bank and he stood up and faced her.

"So you hate me?" he said softly.

He felt the flesh on her arm and she shrank back.

"You loathe me," he said. "And you're afraid of me. Come closer."

She stepped closer. She wanted to turn and dive back into the lake and swim away but his eyes held her. He hissed softly at her.

"After they hang Johnny Price—" he said.

Trelia wasn't very clear about what happened after that. But I know what happened. It was as if I had been there.

Trelia stopped being afraid and she looked straight into the little old man's eyes.

"They won't hang Johnny Price," she said.

"Oh yes they will," the little old man said. "They'll put a rope around his neck and drop him through a trapdoor and a man with a stethoscope will listen to his last heart-beats."

"No they won't," said Trelia.

Then she spoke without thinking of what she was saying or knowing why she said it.

"Because I'm not afraid of you," she said.

The green light blazed up in the little old man's eyes and he reached for her. But Trelia didn't back up and the little old man's hands never touched her. He clutched at her and he stood before her and looked into her eyes. Then he took a backward step.

Trelia walked toward him.

"They won't hang Johnny Price," she said.

The little old man backed away and Trelia stepped closer. The little old man wavered. He looked into Trelia's eyes again and then he stepped backward into the lake.

There wasn't a splash, Trelia said. It was as if the little old man had melted in the black waters. He was gone and Trelia was alone by the edge of the lake and it seemed as if a million tiny living creatures in the forest had come to life and were rustling through the leaves.

42

And so I was out of jail and the little old man was gone for good and I should have been calm and happy but I wasn't. I was at my apartment with Dorgan, changing my clothes and throwing those away that had the smell of the jail on them.

"I've got to see Trelia right away," I said. "But I'm afraid."

"What're you afraid of?" Dorgan asked.

"Of what changes there might be in her," I said.

"The changes in her are what made her beautiful," he said. "Look at that."

He pointed to a canvas on the wall. It was Trelia, a different Trelia. He was right, she was beautiful. She was the most beautiful thing I'd ever seen.

"Is she coming here?" I asked.

"I don't think so," he said. "In fact, I know she won't. She met you at the lake and I suppose that's where you'll find her tonight."

"Maybe after what's happened, after the little old man's death, she's changed again," I said.

"You'll have to find that out for yourself," said Dorgan. "But I wish it was me she was waiting for at the lake."

"I'm going," I said, "but I'm afraid."

I was still afraid, or maybe it was nervousness, when I went to the park and walked down the dark path leading to the lake that night. There was moonlight on the lake but there wasn't any sound and I didn't see Trelia. I waited for an hour and got more impatient and nervous and finally I was about to go away when I heard a splash and I saw Trelia swimming toward me from the other side. She came slowly and when she was near shore she turned on her back and floated and the moonlight was reflected on her white skin.

"Trelia," I said. "Trelia."

She looked at me and for a while she didn't move. Then there was a splash and she was on her feet running through the shallows toward me.

"Johnny," she said, "Johnny Price."

She threw her wet arms around me and pressed her white body against mine and I stroked her damp hair and we couldn't say anything more for a while.

"I'm glad you've come back, Johnny Price," she said finally.

"So am I," I said. "You don't want me to go away again?"

"Not ever," she said.

"I won't," I said. "I won't ever, Trelia."

She sort of sobbed and laughed against my shoulder and I was happy. I was happy but I felt vaguely uncomfortable and I noticed she felt the same way. Finally she drew back and looked at me and all of a sudden she crouched and pulled a branch across her middle.

Then I knew the change in her and it was the same thing that'd made me uncomfortable.

Trelia wasn't naked like a child any more. She was naked like a woman and she knew it and I knew it.

"You turn away," she whispered. "You turn away and don't look, Johnny Price, until I swim over and get dressed."

I turned and after I heard a splash I turned back and saw Trelia swimming swiftly across the lake. Her body was a white, moving blur. Finally she disappeared in the shadows.

43

Trelia and I didn't discuss it. She went home with me as if it had all been arranged. And Dorgan, too, acted as if we'd planned the whole thing and he'd agreed to the arrangement. He said he wanted to do some painting in the mountains and went away.

We were alone and for a while all I could do was to look, at Trelia and tell myself that it couldn't be true that she was there with me and that she loved me.

And then I kissed her and she smiled into my eyes and I ceased being a human being. The beauty and the happiness I had weren't made for men. Trelia's kiss changed me into something else—some sort of forest god who had a perfect right to mate with a water-nymph who had come to him from the black waters of a lake.

That lasted for a week. I don't remember ever going out. I must have eaten but I don't remember it. What was happening to me was like a beautiful pain—something that was so exquisite and keen that a little of it was forever and yet I knew it couldn't last.

And it *will* last forever—even though it was over in a week.

Trelia started to change and I didn't notice it for a while. I felt it and wouldn't believe it until the day I went into a room and Trelia was sunning herself near a window. I came in and stood still and wondered what it was happening to me.

And then it came to me.

Trelia wasn't naked like a woman any more. She was naked like a child. She was like she was when first I knew her. I felt embarrassed and uncomfortable.

She turned and smiled at me.

"Hello, Johnny Price," she said.

"What's the matter, Trelia?" I asked.

Her eyes were puzzled and she hesitated. "It's something in the room," she said.

"Is it this room, Trelia?" I asked. "Or is it *all* rooms?"

She looked away from me.

"I don't know," she said.

I went out and pretty soon she came into the room and I noticed she was staring at the picture Dorgan had painted of her. I looked at it, too, and slowly I realized that there was something the matter with it—it wasn't perfect any more.

I don't mean it'd changed. It hadn't. But Trelia had changed. She didn't look as she did in the picture any more.

I looked at the picture and then at Trelia and the picture began to bother me. It was bothering her, too.

She noticed that I was watching her and she stopped looking at the painting. She went back into the other room and I tried to figure things out; I tried to figure out a way that there wouldn't be anything for me to decide; but I knew sooner or later it would catch up with me.

When Dorgan came in with some canvases under his arm I was glad to see him. A day or so before I would have hated him.

Trelia was in the room and she smiled at him and said hello and then she became silent and looked at the painting on the wall.

Dorgan looked at her and then at the picture.

"I guess that's what I came back for," he said.

He walked over to the painting and took it from the wall.

"It was true then," he said. "But it isn't now."

He threw the painting into the fireplace before I could reach him.

I grabbed his arm.

"Why did you do that?" I asked.

"I think you understand," he said. "I painted her as something she isn't—something she couldn't be."

He pointed to Trelia. She was staring at the burning canvas. As it curled and burst into flame her eyes brightened. She shook her head and looked around her. Suddenly she smiled and spread out her arms.

"I'll go now," she said. "I've been away a long time."

She stood at the door and smiled at me.

"Good-by, Johnny Price," she said.

Then she was gone. I stood still for a minute, thinking of crying out for her to come back and realizing that it wasn't any use. Then I turned to Dorgan.

"You're here," I said, "and you're my best friend, but I'm lonesome. From now on I'll do things with all sorts of people—I'll have crowds around me—but I'll always be lonesome."

The *Manhunt* Stories

Sex Murder in Cameron

February 1953

Old Doc Marston is a stubborn cuss. When they found the body of Cass Buford with his head sliced in the middle by an axe and started looking for Linda, old Doc Marston said that what had happened to Cass didn't surprise him one bit. When they caught Linda hiding in Jim Carver's cabin trying to wash the blood out of her dress, Doc Marston seemed almost disappointed that she hadn't got away. When they remembered that Jim had been hanging around the Buford farm long after his work as handyman was done and that Cass had complained about it, Doc Marston made a lot of enemies by saying that folks were taking too much for granted.

What made the people really disgusted with Doc, though, was Doc's attitude when Linda calmly confessed that she'd killed Cass.

"Maybe she did," Doc said, "but there's more back of it than anybody knows about. There's something mighty strange about this whole business."

"You bet there is," the sheriff told him. "There's something damned strange about a woman who kills a man who gave her such a good home as Cass gave Linda."

"How do you know she had a good home?" Doc asked. "You haven't ever lived with Cass."

"And neither have you," the sheriff said.

That stumped Doc. He didn't have anything to say for a while. Which was a good thing for Doc, because most folks thought he'd said too much already.

Everyone admitted, of course, that there was something strange about Cass' marrying Linda. Cass was one of the most important men in Cameron County. He was the last of the Bufords and he owned everything that was left of the family fortune. It wasn't as much as it used to be, but still there was a well-paying farm and a half interest in the Cameron First National Bank and some first and second mortgages that paid good interest.

Besides all that, Cass was young and good-looking. He had black hair and he was tall and slender and he dressed well. There was something funny about his eyes, though. They weren't exactly crossed, but they were slanted in an odd way. This didn't spoil his good looks, however. The ladies seemed to think it made him more handsome.

Whether it was because he was handsome or because he was rich, the ladies liked Cass. He could pick and choose even when he was a kid. Before he was fifteen there was almost a shooting between the Carrolls and the Bufords over Emily-Sue, the Carroll girl. She was thirteen and she came home one night with her dress torn and her face scratched and said Cass did it. Old man Carroll got a gun and went over to the Buford's and went around and around the house to get a shot at Cass who was hiding underneath.

Finally old man Buford came out and there were some hot words and old man Carroll threatened to shoot him, too. Then they calmed down and got to talking and everything was settled. Mr. Buford loaned Mr. Carroll his prize Hereford bull which old man Carroll had been trying to borrow ever since it won the blue ribbon at the state fair.

After that, Cass didn't get into much trouble. Anyway, he was pretty careful.

It wasn't until he was nineteen that old Doc Marston started hating Cass. It wasn't over very much, either. It was over a dog that wasn't worth a cent. The dog's name was Nero. When people asked Cass what breed Nero was he'd always grin and say it was a cross between a boll weevil and a hook-worm. That always got a laugh.

One day Cass came into the village store laughing. He'd just killed Nero. Something had been killing chickens around the Buford place and Cass decided that it was his dog. So he took him out and killed him.

"I took my twenty-two along," Cass said, "and I drove out near Willow Branch. I got Nero out of the car and let him have it, right between the eyes."

He sat on the counter and reached for a bottle of pop.

"Damnedest thing you ever heard of," he said. "The bullet hit him right between the eyes and he went down like his head'd been chopped off. I started for the car and damned if Nero didn't get up. I aimed again and then the fun started. Around and around the car he went—him with a bullet in his head—and me after him a-hooting and a-hollering so's hell wouldn't have it."

He laughed, thinking of his chasing a dog that was supposed to be dead.

"Finally," Cass said, "he jumped into the car—into the front seat where he always rode—and tried to sit up like nothing had happened and he didn't have a bullet in him."

Then Cass went on to tell how he dragged Nero out of the car and beat him to death with a rock.

"Damnedest thing you ever heard of," he said.

Old Doc Marston walked closer and looked at Cass. He looked a long while, as if he'd never seen Cass before. Then he spat as if he were aiming at Cass' feet.

"Tchew!" he went. "Yes. It *is* the damnedest thing I ever heard of!" Then he turned and walked off.

After that, Doc Marston would hardly ever speak to Cass, even when he treated Cass for measles or flu or a cut hand.

It was about ten years later that word got around that Cass was seeing Linda Wells once in a while. At first, nobody'd believe it. Linda had never had a fellow, not even when she was in grammar school. The plain truth is that she was just about the sorriest looking girl in the whole county. She was tall for a girl, and big-boned, and her body didn't have much more shape to it than a hoe handle. Her mouth was too wide and her eyes were too small and even in the summertime her skin was always a dead white, a sort of fish-belly white. And that wasn't all that was wrong with her. Her teeth weren't in straight and she had straggly hair that no amount of combing or braiding or silk-ribboning would make look like a girl's hair should.

Linda's father was poor and she worked on his farm just the same as a hired hand. She never went to dances and it wasn't very often that she came to church socials. When she did, she stuck in a corner and nobody paid any attention to her except the preacher and his wife.

So when Cass started going around with her, people couldn't figure it out.

"Maybe he's after something," one of the fellows said.

Another fellow laughed.

"He ain't that hard up," he said. "Not that Linda wouldn't be broadminded about it."

"How do you know about that?" he was asked.

"One night after a church social I was gassed up," the fellow said. "I met Linda going home and I started walking along with her. I fooled around a little bit and you shoulda seen how that gal took to it. I bet I was the first guy ever tried anything."

"What happened?" he was asked.

"Well," he said, "it was dark and I figured what the hell!"

He made a face.

"Ugh!" he said. "Even in the dark, and gassed up like I was, I couldn't go it."

He laughed. "Too bad she isn't pretty," he said.

"Well, she ain't and if what I hear's true, Cass Buford's gone off his nut," another guy said.

Off his nut or not, Cass kept on going with Linda and pretty soon it wasn't just a rumor. It was a fact. He took her everywhere, to dances and church socials and skating parties and everything. At first the fellows took it as a joke, but they quit laughing to Cass' face. He beat up a couple of humorists and that ended that. Cass was a powerful man and he had a funny streak in him. When he started fighting it was for keeps, and when he got another man down he'd tear into him and see just how bad he could cut him up with his fists before somebody hauled him off. Sometimes he'd keep hitting another man long after he should have stopped... almost as if he was sort of enjoying it. Guys who'd been in a fight with Cass Buford remembered it a long time.

Nobody believed Cass'd actually marry Linda, though. He was too good-looking and too rich. Every single girl in Cameron County had her cap set for him. He hadn't gone with any of them steady, but everybody thought that that was because he was choosey.

At first they figured maybe Cass wanted some other Cameron girl and she was holding out and that Cass was lugging Linda around to make her jealous.

The preacher's wife thought Cass was just trying to be a good Christian.

"The poor girl's been neglected," she said, "and Cass is just being charitable."

Old Doc Marston spat.

"Tchew!" he went. "Whatever that young whelp's got on his mind, it isn't charity and you can be sure of that!"

And then Cass ups and marries Linda. It was hard to believe, but all of a sudden there was Cass and Linda standing before the preacher and promising to love, honor and obey. Cass was as solemn as a barnful of owls, but Linda couldn't hide her excitement. She had on a pretty dress and, for the first time in her life, she had put paint and powder on her face. Her eyes sparkled and she smiled and squeezed Cass' hand. She was so excited and happy and all that she even looked kind of pretty.

During the ceremony some of the women cried. It was sad and beautiful and wonderful, they said, that such a plain, ordinary, ugly girl as Linda should be made so happy by Cass.

The couple left on a honeymoon and the whole county kept right on talking about the wedding. It was hard to believe, but there it had happened and everything was settled. Nobody in the county ever mentioned that Cass might of got a good wife. It was all Linda and how lucky she was. Everybody figured Cass'd done something noble and fine and generous and everybody liked him a lot more for it.

Everybody but old Doc Marston. He chewed and spat.

"Tchew," he went. "It'll come to no good end. Just you wait and see."

When Linda got off the train from the honeymoon she still had on paint and powder and a pretty dress, but you wouldn't have thought for a minute that she was pretty. She didn't seem any too happy either, but she smiled at everyone and said she'd had a wonderful time.

Everybody noticed how kind and considerate Cass was when he helped Linda into the car. You'd of thought he was a prince or something helping the most beautiful lady in the world into a carriage all lined with silk.

And Cass kept on being kind and considerate. People invited to dinner couldn't believe their eyes when they saw how gentle Cass was with Linda. He kissed her and loved her right before everybody and sometimes he went a little too far with it and shocked some of the ladies.

What puzzled people was the way Linda acted. She didn't bother to use powder or paint any more. She didn't wear pretty dresses, either. When Cass kissed her and loved her in front of people she tried to pull away at first. Then something'd happen to her and her lips'd part and she'd grab Cass' arm and look at him kind of wild until she remembered where she was. Then she'd turn and run out of sight and everybody'd be embarrassed.

That went on for a long time: Cass being kind and considerate and loving Linda a little too much before people and Linda acting funny about it.

And then Cass hired Jim Carver as handy-man. Jim was from another county and he wasn't much good as a farm worker. He was a scrawny, ferrety-looking guy, always grimy and ragged, and most of the time he was either half drunk on sweet wine or sick to his stomach from what he had drunk the night before. He was as shiftless as they come, and nobody liked him. He was just plain no-account, folks said, and the only kind of work he ever got was the hateful odd jobs nobody else would do.

Everybody said it made them feel uncomfortable just to be around him.

Jim didn't live on the Buford farm. He came out from the village about three times a week and did what there was to do. At first he went back to his shack in the village soon's work was over and got drunk. But then he started staying around the farm a little while longer in the evening before he went home, weeding Linda's flower garden and bringing her shoots and things from other gardens.

At first people thought it was just because Linda was kind-hearted. Jim was different from most folks and so was Linda and it was natural they'd have something in common. People didn't pay much attention to the thing at all.

Then a sort of rumor started going around. At first nobody paid any attention to it. Linda was smart enough to know what side her bread was buttered on, they said. She had enough sense not to take any chances ruining the best thing that'd ever happened to her. Besides it was silly. Jim was such a miserable fellow, what with being drunk or sick half the time and all, that he wouldn't appeal even to Linda.

For a while Cass went along just as usual. Then he spoke to just a few of his closest friends and made them promise never to breathe a word of it around. If they did, he said, he'd beat their heads off for them. That's the reason the thing didn't spread as fast as such things usually do. When Cass said he'd beat someone's head off he meant just that.

It wasn't until Cass went to the preacher that things started to happen. He was in the parsonage a long time and when he came out those who saw him didn't suspect that he'd had anything serious on his mind. Remembering it later, they said he'd had a kind of funny smile on his face.

The preacher told about his part later. He said he went to Linda and tried to get her to pray. She wanted to know why and the preacher told her. She acted like the preacher must be crazy. Then he told about the talk he'd had with Cass. Linda didn't seem to believe him at first. He went on talking and scolding her and urging her to pray her sins away and promise to try and live down the ugly, black, slimy sin she'd committed. She just sat there like a hunk of stone and didn't say anything. The preacher went on talking and suddenly Linda got up and ran out of the room crying. The preacher couldn't find her, so he went home and talked to his wife about it.

It was the next morning they found Cass lying in the kitchen with his head split open by an axe. The axe was laying right beside him and the blood on it was beginning to dry. At first they thought it must have been a robbing tramp who did it and then Cass' friends came out and told about what Cass had confided to them. The preacher told his story, too.

That put a different face on things. They started looking for Linda. They found her in Jim's cabin washing a bloody dress. Jim tried to help her out, but the sheriff smashed his face in with one blow and called him all the filthy names he could think of while he lay on the floor with blood spouting between his fingers.

Linda was awfully ugly then. Her hair hadn't been combed and she had on an old faded dress. She looked worse than before Cass married her. She wouldn't talk. She wouldn't cry or she wouldn't look afraid. She was just sullen.

Linda wouldn't talk until they got her to the county jail.

Then she said: "I did it. I hit him with the axe."

They asked her why and she wouldn't answer. She just didn't pay any attention to questions. It didn't matter.

It was the most exciting thing that'd ever happened in Cameron County. Nobody talked about anything else. The more people talked the more excited they got. Everybody remembered what a fine, upstanding, kind and generous man Cass Buford was and all he'd done for Linda. And then she'd killed him out of lust for a no-good bum like Jim. She ought to be lynched, they said.

Somebody suggested that Jim ought to be lynched first and they went for him. But Jim had packed up and gone away. Nobody ever saw him again.

The crowd sort of cooled down while looking for Jim and they didn't make any serious attempt to lynch Linda after that. It was decided that law and order would take its course and there'd be a county hanging in back of the jail just as soon as Linda was found guilty.

The trial attracted a lot of attention in the county and even the big city papers took it up. They said Linda was the Cinderella Girl who'd murdered her fairy prince.

Cameron people didn't call her anything like Cinderella. They called her every low name they could think of. They hated her. When Doc Marston still insisted there was something behind the case other than a depraved woman's lust, people just walked away from him. He was too old a man to beat up. They just put him down as cracked and let it go at that.

The trial was over in a hurry. The defense attorney couldn't do much. Linda wouldn't help him. She just sat there in the courtroom stony-faced and looking straight ahead. She wouldn't even testify.

The county attorney made a longer speech than was necessary, seeing as Linda was practically convicted already. He told of what a loving husband Cass had been, how he'd demonstrated his love before all sorts of people. He spoke of the fine home Cass'd given Linda and how she'd had everything a woman can desire. And then she'd thrown it all away for the lustful love of a man decent people wouldn't even speak to.

"And then," he said, "when her husband found her out she deliberately murdered him so that she could carry on her affair with the other man."

It took the jury five minutes to bring in a verdict of guilty of murder in the first degree and when they led Linda out of the courtroom, the other women spat at her.

The gallows was rigged up in back of the county jail. The crowd began gathering before dawn and by sunrise every man, woman and child in Cameron County was packed into the square. The prisoners in the jail lined the windows to watch.

Just as the sun came up and the roosters started crowing and the early freight began whistling far off on the river bend, they led Linda out of the jail and up the stairs to the gallows. A rustle and a murmur ran through the crowd and then a woman started screaming. Not in fear or horror. She was screaming insults at Linda. Some of the others took it up, but the men looked at one another and at the women and then kept their eyes on Linda and didn't say anything.

Linda's arms were strapped close to her sides and she walked with short, dragging steps and looked straight ahead and didn't seem to see anything, not even the noose dangling before her eyes.

The sheriff asked her did she have anything to say and she shook her head without looking at him. The sheriff gave the signal and the jailers who'd been practicing on a dummy went to work. It was one-two-three—just like a well-executed football play. One man knelt and strapped her legs together. Another put a black bag over her head and another slipped the noose over that. The sheriff waved his arm and the strings were cut and there was a clang like a heavy door slamming and Linda was below the trap and two men were holding her feet, pulling down so's she wouldn't kick.

Old Doc Marston walked up with a stethoscope and opened Linda's blouse and stood there for ten, twelve minutes and during that long wait while you could hear the roosters crowing louder and the train coming closer, five men and a woman fainted. It was the waiting and silence that got them.

Finally Doc Marston put the stethoscope in his pocket and turned to the sheriff and solemnly shook his head.

"Congratulations," he said. "She's dead."

Later the sheriff was in his office with several of the fellows having a little drink on account of the whole thing'd been such a strain on his nerves.

"I don't like to hang people, especially women," said the sheriff, "but this here Linda sure did have it coming to her. To think of a woman with a strong, virile, handsome man like Cass going around and—"

He didn't finish because old Doc Marston came in.

"I just finished examining Linda," he said to nobody in particular.

One of the fellows giggled nervously.

"Was the operation a success, Doc?" he asked.

The others giggled inside their lips. They didn't want to make fun of a dead woman, but the joke was too good to let pass.

"Oh, yes," said Doc. "It was quite a success. Her neck was cleanly broken."

He walked toward the door and turned and looked at the people in the room. He chewed a while and then he spat right on the sheriff's new office carpet.

"Tchew!" he went. "It might interest you to know you've just hanged a virgin."

He turned and closed the door softly and you could hear his footsteps going down the hall.

You could hear his footsteps even after he reached the end of the hall and started downstairs.

Nice Bunch of Guys

May 1953

All the taxi drivers and the fellows who hung around the pool hall would tell you that Marty was a laugh; you should've seen him when the boys got him burnt up about something. He was more fun than a circus, was Marty. Not exactly crazy enough to be put in the nut house or anything like that, just goofy enough to be really pretty darn funny.

He sold papers at the station. They were *Posts* and Marty yelled something that sounded like "Whoa", so all the fellows got a great kick out of yelling "Giddiap! Whoa!" at him and making him mad. He got screwy when they did that. He'd come across the street with his dirty checkered cap pulled down over one side of his face and his twisted mouth all squeezed up into a snarl.

"You old bootleggers," he'd say. "You old bootleggers!" The fellows got a special kick out of Marty calling 'em bootleggers and they'd laugh like anything. "I'm gonna get you," Marty would say. "Just you wait and see. You'd better not make fun of me."

"Aw, gosh! Don't scare us like that," one of the fellows would say, and everybody'd laugh again. Everyone would gather around. There was always a laugh when you had Marty going. He'd lay his papers on the sidewalk and double up his fists. "Wanna fight?" he'd ask. Then everybody'd act afraid and beg Marty not to hit 'em. Of course they weren't afraid. Marty was just a little fellow and any of the fellows could have licked him easy with one hand. They were just kidding him for a laugh. Even Old Ironsides—that's what they called the corner cop— would come by and grin at Marty standing with his fists doubled up and acting like he was a tough guy.

They'd keep on kidding Marty and he'd start squealing like a stuck pig, he'd get so mad. You couldn't understand what he was saying when he got mad like that. Just a lot of cuss words that didn't make sense. And his mouth would froth like he was a mad dog or something.

Then somebody'd act like he really was going to fight Marty. He'd double up his fist and prance around and wiggle his arms and say, "All right, Marty, look out!" and he'd make a couple passes at Marty. "Come on, put 'em up," the fellow would say, "I'm gonna knock your can off." Then Marty'd start whimpering like a little kid. He'd rub his eyes and back away and say, "You'd better not. You'd better not. I'll tell the cops, that's what I'll do." Then he'd grab his papers and run like hell back across the street. Gee, it was funny!

It wouldn't be no time before he'd forget all about it and he'd be walking up and down the station platform yelling "Whoa, Whoa," or something that sounded like that. He sold a lot of papers because people felt sorry for him, I guess. He kept all his money in one pocket and when there wasn't anybody around he'd take it out and count it. He'd count his money seventy times a day. Guess it was the biggest kick he got out of life. And you couldn't get him to spend a nickel. Nobody knew what he did with his money. He was nutty about money.

He was always begging for it. "Gimme a nirkel," he'd say, looking up at somebody. "Aw, go on, gimme a nirkel. Please," he'd say, "go on, please gimme a nirkel." It was funny the way he said nickel. There was something the matter with his tongue and he couldn't talk straight. He'd do anything for a nickel and that's no kidding. He'd do *anything*. Sometimes when the fellows were drunk they'd get Marty in the back room of the pool hall and if you'd been there you'd seen there wasn't anything he wouldn't do for a nickel.

But one of the biggest kicks was when the fellows would kid Marty about his girls. Of course he didn't have any. He was about thirty years old and he had a face like a monkey. His chin sprouted long black hairs that grew far apart and the fellows said he had pig's bristles instead of whiskers. I don't think he ever shaved but the whiskers didn't get any longer. It was funny to think of him having a girl. Gosh, no girl'd even look at him. Even the Mexican woman would chase him away when he'd go to her shack across the tracks and say what the fellows had put him up to saying.

"Hey, Marty," the fellows would say, "who's that hot number we saw with you last night?" And Marty'd grin sly, like he really had been out with a girl, and he'd say, "Nonna yer bursness" or something like that. And they'd say, "Can't you fix it up for us? Gee, she was a hot number. Oh, boy!" Marty'd act real proud like he really could and he'd say, "Naw sir, not youse guys. Not youse guys. T'hell wit' ya."

The funniest thing was when somebody'd ask Marty what he did to the girl. It was a scream. He couldn't even pronounce the word right. "Aw, you never had one in your life," they'd tell him and he'd get mad. "Tha's all you know," he'd say. "Tha's all *you* know." All Marty knew about things like that was what he heard the fellows saying in the pool hall. But you'd thought he did all 'em himself the way he talked.

A girl would go by on the other side of the street and the fellows would whisper, "Hey, Marty, that your girl?" And he'd say, "Sure," and they'd act surprised and say "Gosh, Marty, you ever—?" And he'd wink like he'd seen the fellows do and say, "Yeah, sure." Sometimes the woman would be the banker's wife or the girl that played the organ at the church but Marty'd say sure everytime. It didn't matter who it was, he'd say the same thing. The fellows always got a laugh out of that.

One of the worst things Marty could think to call a guy was a bootlegger. The fellows around the taxi stand used to tell him that George Burke, the lawyer, was going to have him put in jail. Marty'd go white every time you mentioned jail to him. He was goofy, but he liked his freedom more'n anybody you ever saw. So when the fellows'd rib him up about Burke he'd get scared stiff, then crazy mad. He'd go running past Burke's office fast's he could, yelling, "Burke's an old bootlegger! Burke's an old bootlegger! Yeah, Burke's an old dam bootlegger!" Burke was a little red-faced guy and he'd get hopping mad but he never did anything about it. He knew the people would think it was small potatoes for a big lawyer to pick on a half-wit. So he couldn't do anything. Anytime we wanted a boot we'd rib up Marty to go after Burke. You should've seen it.

The fellows all got a kick out of ribbing Marty, but they wouldn't stand for anybody picking on him. One time they told Marty the reporter for another paper was playing dirty tricks on the *Post*, the paper Marty sold. You'd thought Marty owned the *Post* the way he was willing to fight for it. He couldn't read, but he'd get sore as hell if you told him the *Post* wasn't any good. The fellows kept telling Marty this fellow Danny McLeod was scooping the *Post* and things like that until Marty was hopping mad. One day Danny came walking down the street and one of the fellows said, "There's the dirty punk that's been scooping your paper, Marty. Why don't you sock him?" Marty's mouth got twisted worse than ever and he started biting his lips. When Danny got near him he all of a sudden ran out and hit him on the mouth. You could've knocked the fellows over with a feather. They didn't think Marty had guts enough to hit anybody.

Danny's lip was split right down the middle and blood ran down his chin onto his shirt. He doubled up his fists and acted like he was going to sock Marty back and the fellows came closer. Danny didn't sock Marty, though. He just turned and walked away. If he had started to hit Marty the fellows would have piled him. The fellows got a kick out of ribbing Marty but they wouldn't stand for anyone picking on him. They were as nice a bunch of guys as you'd ever find.

After that every time Danny would come by the pool hall the fellows would yell, "Better run, Danny, here comes Marty." Then they'd all laugh and Danny would walk faster. Pretty soon he got so he wouldn't come by the pool hall any more. Danny was all right but he couldn't take a little kidding.

It made Marty cocky as hell. He went around town bragging about how he licked Danny and every time anybody wanted a laugh they'd say, "Hey, Marty, what'd you do to Danny?" and Marty'd stick out his chest and say, "I beat him up. Yeah, I beat him up." It sure made Danny's life miserable for him and it gave the fellows a lot of laughs.

One of the best jokes the fellows pulled on Marty was about Marge, the red-headed girl who worked at the coffee joint next to the station. It was a lulu of a joke and we had more darn fun, only Marty spoiled it. You'd have never thought Marty would do a thing like that but it just goes to show you how screwy he was. The fellows started telling Marty that Marge was in love with him. At first he'd grin and say, "You can't kid *me,* you can't kid *me.* You're jus' kiddin', 'ats all." But the fellows kept it up. "Of course, she likes you, Marty," they'd say. "She's goofy about you.

She *told* us so." "Did she?" Marty'd ask. "Did she, hones'?" and he'd lick his lips and look across at the coffee joint.

"I bet if you bought her some candy she'd fall hard for you," one of the fellows told him one day. "You think so?" Marty asked, all excited. "Sure," the fellow said. "Try it and see." So by God Marty did try it. Marge came walking by on her way to work one night and Marty popped out of the pool hall and stuck a bar of five-cent candy in her hand. "Here," he said, and started giggling. When he giggled his lips got all slobbery and he looked like he was blowing soap bubbles. The bar of candy was all squeezed up and dirty like Marty'd hung onto it in his pocket all afternoon. Gosh, the fellows roared. "Oh, Marge," they said, "who's your boy friend?" Marge's face got red's a beet. "It isn't funny," she said. "He means well. Thanks, Marty," she said, and walked away fast.

And maybe you think the fellows didn't razz Marge after that! "Hey, Marge," they'd yell, "how's your boy friend?" She'd flush and walk faster and it was always good for a laugh. Marty started hanging around the coffee joint when Marge was working and the owner had to kick him out almost every night. Sometimes he'd give her a bar of candy and sometimes it'd be some flowers he'd swiped out of somebody's yard. She'd take 'em so's not to hurt his feelings but the fellows would play like she really was in love with him. Whenever they saw her they'd ask when was she getting married and things like that. Boy, did it burn her up!

Marty got so he thought Marge really was his girl. "Who's your girl, Marty?" the fellows would ask, and Marty would grin sly as the dickens and say, "Aw, *you* know, *you* know," and he'd giggle and bubbles would come on his mouth. Then the fellows would say, "Hey, Marty, we saw you out with another jane last night. What's the idea? Trying to ditch Marge?" Marty'd get all excited and beg 'em not to tell Marge that. Gosh, it was funny how serious he took the thing. "What do you and Marge do when you go out?" the fellows would ask, and Marty'd grin, *"You* know," he'd say, and then he'd lick his lips and look across the street where she worked.

It was the darnedest, funniest thing you ever saw, until Marty spoiled it. You never can tell what a goofy guy'll do and Marty was like the rest of 'em.

One night the fellows were hanging around the taxi stand in front of the pool hall when they heard a woman screaming like she'd been murdered or something. Before they could figure out where it was coming from, Marge came running into the light out of the alley. Her dress was torn and her face was bloody like it'd been scratched. Her hair was down over her shoulders and she looked like she'd seen a ghost or something. Her eyes were bugged out and she didn't seem to see. She just screamed and screamed. Finally Ironsides found out what it was all about and the fellows all ran down the alley. She stood alone on the corner and kept on screaming. It was awful.

The fellows found Marty hiding behind a garbage can, crying. "I didn't mean to do it," he said. "Don't let them put me in jail." When they got him in jail and started asking him questions he acted like a kid that's been caught stealing candy or something. "I won't do it again," he said. He'd wipe his eyes with his fists and spread dirt all over his face. "Did she tell on me?" he'd ask.

Of course they had to send Marty to the nut house at Stockton. They were afraid he'd bust loose again. He bawled like a kid for three days after they told him what they were going to do, until they took him away. What worried him was he'd be cooped up and wouldn't get to go up and down the streets selling papers. The deputy that took him to Stockton said he didn't fight. He just bawled like a kid.

What made the fellows sore about the whole thing was the way Marge acted when she got out of the hospital. You know how women are. You never know what makes 'em click. Marge was that way. She got the notion the fellows were to blame. That's a hot one, isn't it? How could the fellows been to blame when they weren't anywhere near when it happened? It made them mad the way she started treating 'em. When they went into the coffee joint she treated 'em like dogs, wouldn't kid with them or anything. Never so much as a smile or a pleasant word. The fellows started staying away from the place, so the owner canned Marge. You couldn't blame him.

It seemed what Marty did to her and losing her job and all kind of made her screwy herself. Before she left town she met one of the fellows on the street and he told her he was sorry about her losing her job. "If you'd treated the fellows decent," he said, "the boss would of kept you." Well, sir, she scratched his face something awful, and he had to slap her good to make her quit. He wasn't the kind of fellow that hits women, but women haven't got a right to scratch a fellow's face when he hasn't done anything. Old Ironsides, the cop, agreed with the fellow. He told Marge to get out of town or he'd run her out.

The fellows sometimes say how funny it seems without Marty going up and down the streets yelling "Whoa! Whoa!" They sure used to get a kick out of him.

The Faceless Man

June 1953

At one time if anyone had suggested that the residents of Green Valley could conceivably form themselves into a mob, lusting for the blood of a fellowman, I would have called him insane. Now I know better. Green Valley isn't in the Deep South; it's in a midwestern farming state, which proves that lynching isn't a fault of geography but of humanity, and humanity happens to be a family we all belong to no matter where we live. To those of you who have read about lynchings committed in places far from your homes and who have wondered what sort of a person a lyncher is, I have this to say: A lyncher is neither tall nor short, nor young nor old, nor male nor female, and he is faceless, but, under certain given circumstances and under certain given conditions, he is you and you and you and, yes, he is even me.

The chain of events which led the citizens of Green Valley a long way back down the path of evolution toward their original animal state began during the hot, dry summer when their crops were withering and they were worrying about their mortgages and other debts. Henry Rankins gave them something to talk about other than their troubles by taking Claude Warren, an ex-convict, into his home to live with him and help him run his farm. Claude was hardly more than a kid and his crime had not been committed against us nor among us, but he had served eight months in State's Prison and that was enough to set public opinion against him right from the start.

Perhaps the feeling against Claude might have been passive rather than active if it had not been for Orry Quinn. Orry was the third of Pete Quinn's shiftless sons and he had been employed as a farm hand by Henry Rankins until a week before Claude came along. Henry had fired Orry for general reasons of incompetence and, specifically, for having wandered off one evening to see his girl, leaving the cows in the shed restless and in pain from not having been milked. Any other farmer would have done the same thing under the circumstances and nobody would have been perturbed about Orry's being unemployed, a condition which had grown to be more or less chronic with him anyway, had not Orry seized the opportunity to become a self-constituted martyr to social injustice. He claimed he had performed his labors faithfully and well, only to be removed on a trumped-up charge to make room for a felon, an ex-convict and, for all anybody knew, a potential murderer. This story was accepted at face value by most of the younger and more discontented non-working citizens of the community, and even men of substance and intelligence, who normally wouldn't have accepted Orry's sworn oath as to the date of his birth, began to place credence in it. Green Valley was composed of a close-knit group of families and they believed in taking care of their own. Whether or not they sympathized with Orry, they found it hard to understand why Henry Rankins would have passed up an opportunity to give a native son much needed employment in favor of an outsider who happened, in addition, to be a criminal.

Finally a small delegation called at Henry's farm to seek the answer. They found Henry in a shed cleaning eggs and placing them in cartons. Helping him was Claude Warren. Claude was a husky, clean-cut, towheaded kid not much different than dozens of others in Green Valley, excepting that his skin was pale and there was a half-apologetic look in his eyes.

Henry, a small old man with wrinkled, leathery skin, seemed to know why the delegation was there.

"Would you mind taking a walk, son?" he said to Claude. "I think my good friends and neighbors want to have a talk with me."

Claude nodded, then hurried away, his head hanging as if he, too, knew the reason for the visit. Then Henry faced his friends and neighbors.

"Hello boys!" he said blandly. "How're things? How's crops? Been working hard? Been borrowing money from the bank? How much? Got any insurance in case you kick off and leave your families without support?" As he talked, his eyes seemed to be boring into those of each individual member of the group. "How're you getting along with your wives?" he went on. "Any truth to the rumor that one of you slapped his old lady in front of the kids? And how about your daughters? Do you know where they are of nights and what they do?"

He paused and waited as the others shifted their feet uneasily in the dust, avoided his gaze and remained collectively silent.

"You seem to be very uncommunicative today," Henry finally said. "By the way, boys, is there any little thing I can do for you? Do you, by any chance, want to ask *me* a question?"

They glared sullenly and hatefully at him, then turned in a body and walked back to their cars. By the time they had reached the road they had regained their voices and they were muttering angrily among themselves.

Later on, the same delegation called on Sheriff Ben Hodges. They were thoroughly aroused now and they demanded that the sheriff do something about ridding the county of a known criminal who might at any moment turn out to be a menace to the peace and security of them all. Sheriff Ben was a big man and some of his weight was fat. He was well-disposed and given to indolence, being more inclined to sit in his easy chair and read books than militantly and actively to perform the duties required of his office. He had maintained his job throughout the years by giving the appearance of agreeing with everybody about everything and never taking sides in a public controversy. This time, however, he felt that he had to make a stand.

"Well, now," he said mildly, "as for that kid being a menace, I'm not so sure. You see he's a distant kin of Henry's—son of a cousin on his mother's side, I think—and Henry had him pretty thoroughly investigated before he took him in. Claude lived all his life in the city where they burn coal to make steel and the only patch of green he ever saw was in the public park where the police had signs forbidding him to walk on the grass. One hot evening, when the air was moist and full of smoke and soot, some boys his own age drove by in a car. They had girls with them and they took Claude along for a ride in the country. It turned out that the car had been stolen and Claude was convicted of complicity in the crime." Sheriff Ben spoke as persuasively as he knew how, trying to make them understand so's not to have trouble with them. "I know," he conceded, "that Claude probably had sense enough to realize that those other boys really didn't own that automobile, but, still in all, when a kid's hungry for a breath of country air, he isn't going to be too particular how he gets it, is he?"

The delegation didn't understand and what's more, they didn't believe Sheriff Ben's version of Claude's crime. Rumor had given them an uglier and more interesting version and they preferred to believe that. They resented Sheriff Ben's attempt at cleaning up Claude's character. Claude was a criminal, they said, and, if the sheriff wanted to, he could find some sort of a pretext to run him out of the community. The implication was that, if the sheriff appreciated which side his bread was buttered on, he would do what was required of him. Sheriff Ben understood the implication. He had eaten the public's bread for many years and sometimes it had a bitter taste; it was buttered with humiliation. On this day he had no appetite for it, and he made the political mistake of openly antagonizing a group of representative citizens.

"As for being a criminal," he said, "sometimes that's a state of mind and the result of circumstances. I don't suppose that there's many of us here who, at one time or another, couldn't have been in Claude's shoes. During prohibition, for instance, some of you farmers made hard liquor and some of you merchants sold it. Most of us drank it and I, being sheriff, violated my sworn oath by overlooking it." He stared steadily and defiantly at them. "That isn't all I've overlooked," he said, "and some of you wouldn't like it if I got more specific. In any event there're darned few of us who, according to the strict letter of the law and with a little bad luck, couldn't have a prison or a jail record hanging over us."

He rose and waved a heavy hand in dismissal.

"Come to see me again, gentlemen," he said. "As you know, I am always at your services. But the next time you come to me about that kid, who's working ten hours a day for a chance at a decent way of life, I'd appreciate it kindly if you'd have more to go on than your prejudices."

The delegation clumped angrily out of the office and Sheriff Ben realized that he had seriously jeopardized a job that perhaps he didn't deserve and, with it, the money he didn't at all times earn.

After that the citizens of Green Valley sullenly accepted Claude's presence among them. They didn't offer him any physical harm; no individual would have thought of it, excepting Orry Quinn, and he, being a coward, would not have risked the attempt. They simply ignored Claude and, excepting for Henry

Rankins and Sheriff Ben, the kid didn't have a friend or a speaking acquaintance in the community until Laura Hannifer came along. Laura was the only child of one of the oldest families in Green Valley. Her parents had pampered her a great deal and, because she had a will of her own, she was considered arrogant. She had just recently returned home from a visit with relatives in another part of the state, and one day she rode her horse up to Henry Rankins' house and got off and sat on the porch with him.

"Hello, Uncle Hank," she said to Henry, who was no kin of hers, "I just dropped in for a glass of milk and to stick my nose into your business. I understand you're harboring a dangerous criminal hereabouts."

"I sure have," said Henry, grinning at her. "A regular killer-diller."

"Good for you," said Laura. "I've been hearing about him and I understand that the citizens of our community don't like him. Well, anybody these people around here don't like has a long running start toward being my pal. I don't like most of *them,* either."

Then Claude Warren, his face smudged with grease from his working on the tractor, came around the corner of the house and stood staring at Laura as if he'd never seen a girl before. Certainly he'd never seen a girl so healthy and tanned and with such golden hair and with such a friendly look in her eyes.

"Hi, Dirty-face," she said gaily to him. "Come on over and sit a spell." As he stood and goggled at her she laughed at him. "Don't be bashful," she said. "I came over here just to see you. Robbed any interesting banks lately?"

Her grin was so infectious and friendly that he grinned back at her and finally obeyed her command and sat beside her on the porch. Henry departed to get a glass of milk and, when he returned, Laura had already succeeded in thawing Claude out. He was talking to her, a little embarrassed, but with the eagerness of a kid who has long been starved for companionship.

It might have been sympathy and understanding on Laura's part at first, but it soon grew beyond that and presently everybody in Green Valley was discussing the outrageous carryings-on of Laura Hannifer with the ex-convict. The carryings-on weren't very spectacular. After attending a village dance and being frozen cold by the others, Claude and Laura contented themselves with hunting and fishing and riding horses together, and, in order to give Claude time for that, Laura helped him with his chores around Henry's place. The mere fact that Laura kept company with Claude, however, constituted a howling scandal.

Ramsey Hannifer and his wife did their best to break up the affair. At first they pleaded with Laura, and then they threatened all sorts of punishment, but she defied them. She loved Claude, she declared, and she intended to marry him one day. Any interference from them, she told them, would only succeed in hastening the event. They knew her well enough to realize that she meant business. Finally, in the hopes that the whole thing was merely infatuation on Laura's part and that eventually she would come to her senses, they ceased to offer any open opposition to the affair. They had, however, a definite plan of action which they intended to adopt in case the thing went too far.

Other residents of Green Valley did not know of this plan and they were of the opinion that immediate and drastic action should be taken to end what they considered to be an intolerable breach of public morals. There was some talk of forming a citizens' committee to remove Claude forcibly from the community, but it is doubtful if anything would ever have been done about it if, one afternoon, Henry Rankins had not been found dead in a pool of blood on the floor of his barn. Jason Watters, the county tax assessor, who discovered the body, did not bother to investigate the cause of death. He ran from the barn and called for Claude and discovered that Claude was nowhere in sight and that, in addition to this Henry's car was missing. Jason telephoned Sheriff Ben and then proceeded along the road to town, spreading the word that Henry Rankins had been murdered and that Claude Warren had disappeared.

By the time Sheriff Ben arrived at the farm, a dozen cars were parked in front of it and the barn was filled with men who milled in a circle about the body and disturbed or destroyed whatever evidence there might have been. This had not prevented them from forming opinions, however. They had picked up and handled and passed around various instruments, one of which they were certain had been used to crush Henry's skull, and they were in disagreement only as to which was the true weapon. Even if Sheriff Ben had been an expert, which he wasn't, he could not have gained much information from conditions as he found them. He ordered the others out of the barn and then telephoned Doc Doran, the coroner, to come get the body.

By the time Sheriff Ben came out of Henry's house after making the phone call, the crowd in the yard had doubled and they were excitedly discussing a new aspect of the case. Laura Hannifer, it had been learned, had also disappeared. Her worried parents didn't know her whereabouts, but they were afraid that she might have eloped with Claude Warren. This was all the crowd needed to know. They scattered to their cars and the search for Claude and Laura was on.

Sheriff Ben went back to his office and waited. It was not long before Lonnie Hearne, his deputy, assisted by Orry Quinn and another volunteer posseman, came in, dragging Claude and Laura with them. Claude had evidently resisted arrest and he was considerably banged up and bloody about the face. Laura, whose clothes were torn, was breathing fire and defiance and still struggling in the arms of the two possemen.

"Caught 'em with the goods," Lonnie announced proudly. "They were in Henry's car and Claude had a pocketful of money that he didn't earn as no farm hand."

While Lonnie prodded Claude with his revolver, the two kids told their story. They had discovered that Laura's parents had been secretly planning to send her to California to live with relatives, and, aided and abetted by Henry, they had decided to get married. Henry, they claimed, had lent them his car and the money for the elopement and the last they had seen of him he was in good health. They had not known, they declared, that Henry was dead until Lonnie and the others arrested them.

"And that's the truth, so help me," said Claude.

"It's a damn lie and, this time, *nobody's* going to help you," said Lonnie, viciously jamming the revolver against Claude's spine.

"Up until the present moment," said Sheriff Ben, knocking the revolver out of Lonnie's hand, "you're neither judge, jury, nor executioner for this commonwealth, Lonnie. You, Orry, let go of that girl and all of you clear out. I'll take over from now on."

After the others had made a reluctant departure, Sheriff Ben turned to Claude.

"Maybe you're telling the truth," he said. "I don't know. Anyway, I'm going to lock you up until we get a better idea of what the truth is."

Following a struggle with Laura, who insisted on being locked up too, Sheriff Ben succeeded in placing Claude in a cell. Then he sat and talked with Laura until her parents arrived and, after a great deal of difficulty, persuaded her to go home with them.

At first there were only a dozen men in front of the jail. They stood around and talked angrily but without purpose. Orry was one of them. After awhile he detached himself from the group and went into the village where he found a cluster of citizens gathered in front of the hotel discussing the case. He shoved his way into the center of the cluster and soon dominated the conversation by boastfully telling of his part in the capture and subjugation of Claude Warren, the murderer.

"How do you know he's a murderer?" someone asked. "Did he confess?"

"Well," said Orry, hesitating a moment, "not in so many words, but he *practically* did."

Then Orry went about the village and told his story to other groups of eager listeners, embellishing it as he went along. By the time he had reached the end of the main street he had dropped the word *practically* from his narrative. Claude, according to his story now, had *actually* confessed to having beaten Henry Rankins to death for his money. The news swept back up the street and presently even those who had heard Orry's first version of the story, were convinced that Claude had admitted his guilt.

"And what's more," Orry said importantly to a new group of listeners, "they're not going to let him get away with it. There's talk of breaking into the jail and stringing him up."

Soon word flashed through town and into the farming district that a crowd had gathered in front of the country jail for the purpose of lynching Claude Warren. This story in itself created the crowd which previously had not existed. Men, women and children flocked into the square facing the jail and waited expectantly for something to happen. Nothing happened. The crowd had no purpose or direction and they lacked leadership. Each individual member of the throng considered himself not a potential participant in whatever was about to take place, but merely a spectator to what the others were going to do.

An hour passed and it began to grow dark and the crowd grew more and more restless. They were in the mood of an audience that has paid out good money to see a show, the opening curtain of which has been delayed too long. If they had been in a theatre they would have stamped their feet and whistled. As it was they milled about and looked questioningly at one another and began to murmur, at first petulantly and then angrily. Finally, the shrill piping voice of a small boy rose above the murmur: *"We want Claude Warren!"* Others eagerly picked up the cry and, as they began to roar in unison, they ceased to be individuals and became a mob.

Inside his office, Sheriff Ben sat at a desk with three loaded revolvers before him. He opened a box of shells and began to load a shotgun. Lonnie, the deputy, was nervously pacing the floor.

"You're not going to be fool enough to resist them, are you, Ben?" he asked.

"Can you figure out anything else to do?" asked the sheriff.

"It's crazy," said Lonnie. "They'll tear us to pieces. I ain't going to risk my life for no lousy killer. That ain't what I'm being paid for as a deputy."

"And you're not a deputy any more," said Sheriff Ben. He ripped the badge off␣Lonnie's shirt front, unlocked the door and shoved him out. "Now go howl with the rest of the jackals."

He locked the door again and went back and sat at his desk. He listened to the growing roar from outside and he began to tremble and the palms of his hands were moist. In electing Ben Hodges sheriff, the citizens of Green Valley had not bestowed on him superhuman courage. Sheriff Ben was afraid.

The mob had now achieved purpose and direction and it was not long before they obtained leaders. The people of Green Valley had long looked to certain men for leadership in politics, civic enterprises, and church affairs. It was only natural that, in this current project, they looked to the same men for guidance. And those men, out of long habit, accepted the responsibility. Orders were given and eagerly obeyed and soon a heavy timber had been produced and was aimed as a battering ram at the door of the jail.

"Sheriff Ben," yelled Dolph Hardy, one of the leaders, "we'll give you one last chance to deliver Claude Warren before we come in after him."

There was a moment of waiting and then the door opened and Sheriff Ben appeared. Orry Quinn, who was in the forefront of the mob, yelled an obscenity at him and the Sheriff made a move toward him. Orry scurried back into the crowd.

"If I lay my hands on you, Orry," said the sheriff, "I'll slap your face to pulp." Then he looked over the mob. "I am quite willing, however," he said, "to discuss matters with responsible members of this community."

"Cut out the talk." said Dolph Hardy. "We want Claude Warren."

The mob surged forward but Sheriff Ben held his ground.

"Who said you couldn't have Claude Warren?" He held out his hands placatingly. "Take it easy, boys," he urged. "I'm a reasonable man." As the men in front fell back a little and stared expectantly at him, Sheriff Ben continued to speak in a soothing voice. "The thing is," he said, "I don't want any mob tearing through my jail and ripping things apart. This is your own property and if you destroy it, you'll have to replace it out of your own pockets."

At this there was an angry, impatient murmur from the mob. The sheriff held out his hands for silence.

"I'm not saying you can't have Claude Warren," he declared. "I'll deliver him to whichever one of you wants to come in in an orderly and decent manner to get him." He looked at Dolph Hardy. "How about you, Dolph? You've been hollering your head off for him. Supposing you come in and get him?"

Dolph gave the sheriff a startled look and tried to press himself back into the mob. The others urged him on, however, and finally and reluctantly he came up the steps toward the sheriff. Sheriff Ben shoved him inside and then locked the door.

"There he is," Sheriff Ben said to Dolph, pointing to a corner of the office. "He's all yours."

Dolph turned and faced Claude Warren, who was sitting in a chair, his wrists bound by handcuffs and his face swollen and discolored from the beating administered by his captors. Claude looked up at Dolph and his eyes were alive with hopeless, helpless terror. Dolph stared into those eyes and then his mouth dropped open and he shifted his feet and seemed to be at a loss as to what to do next.

"Funny thing, Dolph," said the sheriff musingly, "but Claude looks a lot like your youngest son, Willie, doesn't he? Same size and age. Want to sock him a couple of times before you deliver him to the mob, Dolph? Go right ahead. He can't hit you back, he's handcuffed."

Dolph cringed and turned his face away from the look of animal fear in Claude's eyes.

"Better yet," said Sheriff Ben, placing his hand on Dolph's arm. "Why don't you kill him right here and now, Dolph?"

Dolph stared unbelievingly at Sheriff Ben and began to back toward the door.

"Why not?" asked Sheriff Ben. "You were so all-fired bloodthirsty a while ago. You were willing to *help* kill Claude. Do you mean to say you haven't got the courage to do the job all by yourself? And, look, Dolph, if you do, someday those people out there will be awfully grateful to you. If they kill Claude collectively tonight, someday they're going to have to answer for it individually to whatever God they believe in and, if they happen to believe in hell, why, they're going to have to roast for it. If you take sole responsibility, Dolph, think what a terrible load you'll lift from the conscience of your neighbors in Green Valley."

He took Dolph by the elbow and led him over to the desk where the guns were.

"Would you like to shoot him, Dolph?" he asked. "Help yourself. Which do you prefer—a shotgun or a pistol?" As Dolph stared in horror at the array of weapons, Sheriff Ben opened a drawer and picked up a blackjack. "Or maybe you'd rather take this and beat his brains out," he said.

He extended the blackjack toward Dolph and Dolph stepped back, his face beaded with perspiration and his eyes sick with dread.

"Of course," went on Sheriff Ben, "your original intention was to hang him, wasn't it?" He turned and looked about him. "Now, let's see," he said, "where can I find a really good sturdy rope?"

Dolph turned from him and rushed to the door, clawing at the lock with shaking hands. Sheriff Ben unlocked the door for him and shoved him out into the opening in the face of the tensely expectant mob.

"It seems," said Sheriff Ben in a loud voice, "that Dolph doesn't want Claude Warren any more."

Dolph looked over the mob and it seemed that suddenly he hated every individual in it.

"Go home, you fools!" he cried. "He's only a kid!"

And then his large shoulders shook with sobs and he stumbled into the mob, pushing aside or striking at anyone who stood in his way and crying out loudly for all to go home.

The stunned mob milled about uncertainly for awhile, and then the rumor started and swept through the ranks that, in an adjoining county, the real murderer of Henry Rankins had been captured and was being held in jail. The mob became a group of shamefaced individuals and the individuals hurried from the scene as if fleeing from some nameless terror. Soon the square in front of the jail was deserted.

Of course the rumor that had dissipated the mob was as unfounded as the one that had created it, but, later that night, Doc Doran, the coroner, came into the office and found Sheriff Ben sitting at his desk, now cleared of weapons.

"I just finished the autopsy on Henry," Doc announced. "He died of heart failure. He must have been pitching hay up in the loft when the stroke hit him and, in falling, he sustained those head injuries." Doc looked curiously at the sheriff, who seemed not to be listening to him. "Say, what's this I hear about a mob forming in front of this place?"

"They went home," said Sheriff Ben. "Their kids were sleepy."

Sheriff Ben sat slumped over his desk long after the coroner had left. He had, he realized, no more reason to be proud than any member of the recent mob. At first, in his abject fear of personal harm, he had wanted to hand Claude Warren over to the mob. Then he had decided that, no matter what he did, his days as sheriff of Green Valley were ended and his fear had turned into blind, unreasoning hatred and he had felt the urge to turn his guns on the mob and to kill as many of them as possible, not in the interests of justice, but to avenge himself against the others for having placed him in such a predicament. He had been spared having to make a choice between the two alternatives only because, out of his desperation, a third expedient had occurred to him.

That is why I say to you that a lyncher is neither tall nor short, nor young nor old, nor male nor female, and he is faceless, but, under certain circumstances and conditions, he is you and you and you and, yes, even me.

I am Ben Hodges.

Noir classics from

Staccato CRIME

Bodies Are Dust P. J. Wolfson
"Plenty of hard edged banter, muscular prose and clever riffing on jazz melancholy in this cruel and poignant tale . . . despair that rings so true it hurts."

—Paul Burke, *Crime Time*

I Was a Bandit Eddie Guerin
"Colorful language keeps the pages turning . . . True crime fans will welcome this memoir by a forgotten but once famous criminal."
—*Publishers Weekly*

Round Trip/Criss-Cross Don Tracy
" . . . you won't be disappointed. A tour de force of noir magic."

—Larque Press

Grimhaven Robert Joyce Tasker
"A notable, a keen and intensely moving account of what happens to a man in prison . . ."

—*New York World*

Fully Dressed and in His Right Mind Michael Fessier
"It's one of those books that can affect readers in so many different ways . . . I found it sublimely mysterious and fantastically satisfying."
—J. F. Norris, *Pretty Sinister Books*

How to Commit a Murder Danny Ahearn
" . . . a truly dangerous book . . ."

—*Lansing State Journal*

Fiction and true crime from the Jazz Age—only $12.99 each.

Stark House Press, 1315 H Street, Eureka, CA 95501
Available from your local bookstore, or order direct via our website—
www.starkhousepress.com.

CPSIA information can be obtained
at www.ICGtesting.com
Printed in the USA
LVHW060727040623
748833LV00026B/403